# BIG BOY

DAVID A. ESTES

Paperback-Press
an imprint of A & S Publishing
A & S Holmes, Inc.

ISBN-13: 978-1-945669-72-9

# INTRODUCTION

January 1, 1863, President Abraham Lincoln's Emancipation Proclamation decreed that all slaves on the Southern plantations be set free. Even so, the degradation they suffered before the war survived the devastation of the Southland. Fleeing by the thousands, the freedmen carried with them little more than hope for a better life in a place called Nicodemus.

Nicodemus, Kansas, a monument to the struggle, stamina, and resolve of former slaves to establish themselves as an entity apart, to prove they could stand alone as a culture, a society, as American as the Declaration of Independence. Battered by harsh snowstorms and bone-chilling winds, scorching heat and drought, with dogged grit and determination, the freedmen persevered. They refused to yield to hunger, disease, and grasshopper infestation. They planted seeds with no promise of rain to help them grow, and hauled water from the river to save their crops.

Nicodemus is a proud testimony to "life, liberty, and the pursuit of happiness" under grueling circumstances on the plains of Northwest Kansas. Compelled by the need to make their own way, on a piece of ground never pierced by the blade of a plow, they attacked the frozen soil with hoes, shovels, pick axes, and an unflagging will to grow beans, corn, and potatoes where before only weeds and buffalo grass survived.

Through it all, they injected life into the waterless prairie. Thriving on optimism that something good would come of their labor, feeding on their faith in a merciful God to not be denied the independence they sought, they created freedom they sought in the all-black community of Nicodemus.

The former slaves, lured to Nicodemus by land agents' promises of functioning institutions on the banks of the Solomon River, discovered no such institutions. They went to work building them with their own sweat and strain. They transformed a stretch of nothingness as far as the eye could see into a bustling community of seven hundred souls.

By the 1880's, out of the desolate prairie rose thirty-five places of business, including a bank, newspaper, hotel, a livery stable, churches and a school.

Suffering the attrition of time, and young people's restlessness to seek their fortunes in the cities, Nicodemus today is home to fewer than a dozen families. Still, their roots reach back to their settler forebears of the 1870's. They long ago squelched the notion of attaching "home" to any place besides Nicodemus. Every July hundreds of black people from all over America come swarming back to celebrate "Homecoming."

Neither time nor dust nor fading memory can mitigate the heroism of the dedicated pioneers who came seeking a piece of ground to which they could attach their names and proclaim, "This is mine!" With backbreaking toil, boundless courage and pride, they carved freedom and dignity from what for untold ages was worthless wasteland, and made it into the fertile "promised land" of Nicodemus.

To that land of promise, in the spring of 1877, a former slave named Jeremiah Higgins journeyed in search of his wife and sons whom he last saw when he was traded for a mule.

# CHAPTER ONE

*"I'm free! I'm free!"*

Jubilation swept the Southland like dust in a whirlwind. Negroes by the thousands flung aside their hoes and shovels, scythes and cotton-gathering baskets. They cast off the shackles of slavery and deserted the fields. Shouts of "I'm free!" resounded across the rice paddies and cotton fields from Charleston to Vicksburg, and praise for "Mr. Lincoln" and "Mr. Grant" filled the air.

In the middle of a cotton field, Jeremiah Higgins paused, and folded his calloused hands on top of his hoe handle. Awe-struck by the pandemonium exploding around him, he rested his chin on his hands and watched, trying to take in what his eyes and ears were asking him to believe.

Free? Born into slavery thirty-seven years before, Jeremiah stood six-feet-six, sturdy as an oak stump. For thirteen years he longed for the day when he could go in search of his wife LouEtta, and their sons Joseph and Jacob. Maybe now he could.

Out of the celebration erupting like a geyser all around him, Jeremiah grabbed the word "free." It stood out like a bale of cotton in a wagon load of green beans. He had never been free, though three times he tried for a taste of freedom when he ran away from Massa Logantree's plantation. Each time, the bulldozers chased him down and hauled him back in chains. They locked him in "the box" and fed him three biscuits and one cup of water a day. If "free" meant what he hoped it meant, Jeremiah could now go where he wanted, and look for his family without asking anybody if it was all right.

He rested his chin on his hoe handle and wept.

# CHAPTER TWO

*The surrender*

It was the home of Wilmer McClean at Appomattox Courthouse, Virginia. McClean fled there from Manassas to escape the Civil War. His living room was now the site of General Robert E. Lee's deepest humiliation.

For four years Lee survived the ravages of a war many believed never should have been fought, a war paid for with the blood and sacrifice of six hundred thousand courageous men and untold millions in property loss. But for Lee, the hour he spent waiting for the arrival of Ulysses S. Grant was the most grueling of them all.

President Lincoln's Emancipation Proclamation decreed that all slaves be set free. Even so, for the millions of slaves on the southern plantations, freedom was only a dream until April 9, 1865, the day Lee, Commander of the Army of the Confederacy, surrendered to Grant, the Union Army Commander.

For Lee's army, the end began two weeks earlier when his tattered troops sloshed through ankle-deep mud, eluding annihilation by the tightening vice of the Union army. Food and munitions all but dried up. Union forces severed supply lines to Richmond, and Lynchburg's stores of food and troop replacements were beyond reach. Lee had ordered General George Pickett to make a stand at Five Forks outside Petersburg to defend the vital South Railroad and White Oak Road. The strategy aborted when General Phillip Sheridan mounted a Union strike against the two-mile Confederate front.

Pickett reacted by withdrawing his forces from Five Forks to defend against Sheridan's onslaught, exposing the right flank of the Confederate line.

Grant took advantage of the weakened Southern defenses and ordered an attack along all Confederate lines.

Many of the bedraggled rebels fled in disarray. Some simply walked away and went home. Union forces gained control of the South Railroad, and the Civil War was virtually over.

To the Union commander, Lee grudgingly dispatched a lieutenant on horseback bearing a white flag of surrender. As recently as yesterday, Lee mapped an offensive that would have put Appomattox Village behind him. It also would have opened supply lines to Lynchburg and critically needed provisions, as well as access to fresh troops to bolster his dwindling fighting force. His strategy was negated by the relentless Union assault.

Never in the presence of the Confederate commander was the word "surrender" uttered. Though forced at times to pull back to a more tenable position, Lee would accept no result short of complete victory for the South. Surrounded by Union cavalry and artillery, however, to salvage the remnants of his army, Lee was left with no choice but to yield.

And so it was that General Robert E. Lee, scion of an aristocratic Virginia family, was subjected to the agony of agreeing to terms set forth by the victorious Grant.

Yielding to the inevitable in no way diminished Lee's strength of character, his devotion to the cause of the Confederacy, nor the richness of his Southern heritage. Except for the risk of more bloodshed, and the sacrifice of sons of the South, he would have fought to the death to preserve the right of the Confederacy to live by its own rules.

Lee knew but little of Grant's background. West Point, of course. And, twenty years before, he and Grant served together briefly in Mexico. Before Lincoln summoned him to command the Union army, Grant had retired to a farm outside St. Louis. Slovenly, some called him, and a drunkard. Nonetheless, Lee conceded, Grant's military prowess crushed his Confederate army, and preserved the Union for Lincoln.

Face-to-face with Grant, Lee would accord him the respect he would expect from a fellow officer. By no means, however, would he humble himself in the presence of the victor. He was defeated by the might of greater manpower, not by the weakness of his purpose. The cause of the Confederacy Lee revered as just and honorable. He owned no slaves, but deemed the white man superior to the black, and defended the right of Southern landowners to hold slaves.

Pacing the squeaking wooden floor of the McClean parlor, Lee peered out the rain-spattered front window, scarcely aware of staff officers who accompanied him there. His most difficult task, commending his men for their service to the Confederate cause, and he shared the anguish of failure he saw etched on their haggard faces.

In defeat as in victory, they honored General Lee with utmost respect. He was their commander. As he rode past on his way to Appomattox Courthouse, they paid him tribute with sharp salutes at rigid attention.

Grant's arrival sparked a moment of tension. Neither he nor Lee knew how the other might react under such circumstances. When the Union commander entered the room, drenched head to toe, boots covered with mud to his knees, every Confederate officer snapped to attention with a brisk salute. They awaited Grant's almost embarrassed, "At ease, gentlemen."

Grant saluted General Lee, extending his hand in a cordial greeting. "I remember you, General Lee, from Mexico."

Lee remembered him too, but was in no frame of mind to exchange recollections of times past. It was not a time for pleasantries. Nor was the Southern commander eager to engage in idle conversation with a man he hardly knew. At fifty-eight, Lee was sixteen years older and six inches taller than Grant.

The ruddy-faced Union commander reflected no hint of arrogance nor superiority that a younger man might display in similar circumstances. In fact, Lee later recalled that Grant was magnanimous in their negotiations.

Grant delayed the inevitable by commending the Confederate commander for his outstanding service record. Reminiscing about mutual friends, some of whom were in the room, Grant's intent was to make the surrender as painless as possible for the Southern commander.

Lee's respect was limited to his regard for a fellow officer, the strategist who defeated him on the field of battle. Humility was an emotion he reserved for his relationship to God. His terse response to Grant's outlined terms of surrender was to demand those terms be recorded on paper.

Grant graciously complied.

The Union commander allowed the men of the Confederacy to ride their mounts home and permitted the officers to keep their side arms.

With Lee's surrender, except for a few minor skirmishes, the Civil War was over. No longer was heard the chilling swish of the cannonball, nor the crack of rifles as brother faced brother from opposite banks of a stream. Stemmed was the flow of blood, as both North and South suffered immeasurable loss of life and property. Neither could boast of gain.

Five million slaves were set free, but the bitterness wrought by the Civil War simmered long after the sorrowful sound of the bugler's Taps echoed for the last time across the ravaged land.

# CHAPTER THREE

Jeremiah Higgins knew nothing of the strategy, the disappointment, nor the agony of defeat, of the devastating war. But he knew it was over. No longer would he be shackled hand and foot as a runaway slave.

Somewhere out there beyond the borders of the plantation, his family waited, and somehow he would find them.

Jeremiah was eight years old when Massa Logantree raped and murdered his mother. The boy was then moved into the cabin of Aaron and Hedelvah, who had four children of their own. One of them was a six-year-old LouEtta. LouEtta would one day become the wife of Jeremiah Higgins.

On his fourteenth birthday, already over six feet tall and physically sleek as a thoroughbred, Jeremiah became an aide to Aaron in the blacksmith shop. He repaired harness and wagon wheels, and shod horses. He learned to turn a slab of raw metal until it was hot enough to pound into a plow share, hoe or shovel. He learned by watching Aaron do it and by doing it himself.

Jeremiah didn't know that one day those skills would serve him well on his journey west in search of his wife and sons.

One thing Jeremiah didn't learn. Like many thousands of other freed slaves, he didn't know how to cope with the new freedom suddenly thrust upon him.

A hard-working black man like Jeremiah was a valuable asset, and some slaves were treated well by their masters. Given the choice of leaving or staying on the plantations after the war, many chose to stay rather than face the uncertainty of a freedom they never knew. Most of those who remained were assigned the same jobs they did before. Others, like Jeremiah, suddenly released from the only way of life they knew, sought places far from the plantation to settle, put down roots, and start a new life.

The freedmen's basic skills were as field hands, smithies and yard men. As such they were encouraged by a man named Benjamin "Pap" Singleton, a former slave from Tennessee, to buy land and produce their own crops. But few of them had money to buy land, and those who did were hampered by the landowners' refusal to sell them land fertile enough to produce crops.

Jeremiah lived for the day when he could venture beyond the boundaries of the plantation, with no wish to work a plot of ground the white planters didn't want.

His mission was to find his family. He trudged the length and breadth of Mississippi, leaving behind scraps of worn shoe leather, seeking news of LouEtta and the boys.

After thirteen years of his fruitless searching in the Southland, Jeremiah found himself in a line of black people eagerly waiting to buy tickets for a boat ride up the Mississippi River to St. Louis. He'd heard of St. Louis, as he'd heard of heaven and God. He knew no one who ever went to heaven, nor did he know anyone who had been to St. Louis. He could only imagine it was a big city filled with bright lights and happy people. Next to New Orleans, St. Louis was where most freedmen wanted to go when they died in case heaven was full. He marveled that he soon would be on his way there, and from there to "the promised land" called Nicodemus.

Trudging the state with deathless hope, he didn't find his family in Mississippi. Would they be waiting for him when he got to Nicodemus? How long would he have to wait to find out?

The steamboat ride up the Mississippi from Vicksburg to St. Louis cost four dollars.

Big, broad-shouldered Jeremiah joined the throng of black people scrambling up the gangplank to board the steamer "Joe Kinney," on the first leg of a journey that would end when he got to Nicodemus.

Jeremiah never ventured beyond the borders of the state of Mississippi.

He was fascinated by the roar of the big river's muddy waters tumbling south. He wondered where it was going, and how long it would take to get there, with no notion what awaited him once the boat docked at St. Louis. Even so, having walked countless miles in search of his family, for him the big city would be a brief stop on his way to Kansas.

He elbowed his way up the gangplank, jostled by people as eager as he to get aboard. From somewhere behind him he heard a man's voice, abrasive as a foghorn.

"Hey you, big boy!" the voice bellowed.

With apprehension born of a lifetime of responding to the white field boss's gruff orders, the sea of black faces turned toward the dock. There they saw a skinny white man with a red nose and sharp chin waving his arms.

Jeremiah swallowed hard. Standing head and shoulders above the crowd, along his spine swept a shiver of apprehension. The man was pointing at him. What had he done? What did the man want? It was fifteen years since Mr. Lincoln's freedom paper said all slaves were free. Still, he cringed at the sound of the man's commanding voice.

"Yeah, you, big boy!" the man shouted. "Come on back down here."

Jeremiah pushed his way against the press of the crowd, puzzled as to why he was called back. Was the man going to tell him he couldn't board the "Joe Kinney"? Were his hopes of finding his family going to end half way up the gangplank of the boat that was supposed to take him to the Promised Land?

He pulled up in front of the man sitting on a wooden stool behind a small table beside a bale of cotton. He cast a worried look at the man who called him back. On the table sat a black tin box with the lid open. Inside the box Jeremiah saw a jumble of small green cardboard tickets.

"You got a ticket?" the man said.

A ticket? Jeremiah was puzzled.

"I can't let you go if you got no ticket."

Jeremiah breathed a deep sigh. All he wanted was his ticket? He dug a hand into a pocket and came out with a small square of green cardboard like the ones he saw in the tin box. When he bought the ticket, nobody told him someone else would take it from him before he boarded the boat.

Jeremiah held out the ticket. The man took it and tossed it into the black box.

"Move along now," he said. "No stragglers here."

Jeremiah offered him a relieved nod, and rejoined the crowd edging its way up the gangplank of the "Joe Kinney."

How many other obstacles would fall across his path before he got to Nicodemus?

# CHAPTER FOUR

Plans for a settlement of former slaves on the Kansas plains originated with a man named W. R. Hill. Hill was motivated by the potential aspects of the Homestead Act passed by the U. S. Congress in 1862. The Act provided for the purchase of government-owned public land for five dollars an acre.

Hill also was confident the tracks of the Continental Railroad would reach as far west as Kansas, enhancing his enthusiasm for developing an all-black community there. He left his native Indiana in the summer of 1876 and staked out hundreds of acres of land along the banks of the Solomon River in Graham County, Kansas.

Hill revealed his plans to a group of former slaves who settled in Topeka. He encouraged them to share the news with their friends and relatives who might be looking for a place to make a new start. Hill distributed fliers throughout the South describing Nicodemus as "the new Eden" and the "promised land". He hired agents who traveled to Kentucky, Tennessee, and Mississippi, where they proclaimed the wonders of life on the Kansas frontier.

Black people were lured from the Southland by the promise of "forty acres and a mule" and money enough to live on until their crops came in. The freedmen viewed Nicodemus as a haven where they could become landowners and pointed their hopes toward the unfamiliar west.

In the Spring of '63, Jeremiah was traded to a planter in a distant part of Mississippi.

Separated from his family, he lived for the day when again he could fold his sons Jacob and Joseph in his arms and feel in the night the warm closeness of his wife, LouEtta. Endless days, weeks, and months turned into years he trod the state of Mississippi. He wrapped his feet in burlap to cover holes worn in his shoes, determined that somewhere, somehow, he would find his beloved family.

His search led him to Vicksburg, where he spotted a red-and-white striped barber pole. He wrapped his arms around it to catch his breath, and prayed to the God of his mother for strength to stay on his feet and continue his quest.

On that sweltering afternoon in August of 1878, the weary traveler straightened himself, and mopped his sweat-beaded brow. He was about to relax his hold on the barber pole and walk away when through the barber shop's open door he heard a man's booming voice, and the words "Nicodemus" and "the promised land."

The only promised land Jeremiah ever heard of was the one the preachers went on about, the one God wouldn't let Moses into because of what he did about the water from that rock.

Jeremiah peeked around the barber pole and saw in the barber's chair a hulk of a man with bushy eyebrows, a frowzy graying beard, and a handlebar mustache. The man stepped down from the barber chair, brushed himself off, and handed the barber some money.

"Well now, Mr. Bridges," Jeremiah heard the barber say. "I guess we won't be seeing you around these parts again for a while."

"Not for a while," Bridges said. He was dressed in a gray suit and black boots so shiny Jeremiah thought he could have seen himself in them. "I'll be going back out to Kansas with another bunch of black folks for Mr. Hill."

"I hear the planters are chewing rocks about all those blacks moving out and leaving them high and dry."

"Oh, the planters are, yeah. They're madder than a bushel of bumble bees. Of course, the Democrats are doing everything they can to keep the nigras from leaving, but there's not much they can do about it. Lincoln turned them loose, Lee tossed in the towel, and that fairly well wrapped it up."

"What I hear, that's pretty rough country out there. Kansas, is it?"

Bridges nodded. "It's not bad though. Mr. Hill built me a fine home out there a while back. And

I've got me a woman who takes good care of me." With a wink, he said, "I guess you know what that means."

"Oh yeah," the barber said with a chuckle. "I know what that means all right."

"And I've handled nigras before, you know, so it's not much different from working a bunch of plow horses."

The barber thought that was funny and laughed at it.

Bridges lifted his hat off a wall peg and waved to the barber as he left. He swept past Jeremiah as though he weren't there.

Being ignored by white folks was no bother to Jeremiah. Mr. Lincoln said he was no longer a slave, but black people were still looked down on as if they were something to be ground under boot heels. Born into slavery, degradation was a part of Jeremiah's heritage.

Before he was moved to Aaron's blacksmith shop, Jeremiah trudged up and down the furrows behind a mule-drawn plow or filled his straw basket with cotton till his fingers bled, lacerated by the sharp spears of the cotton bolls.

He was five years old when he picked cotton with his mama the first time. He worked ahead of her along the same row. He stuffed his pockets with the fluffy cotton, raced back and unloaded them into her basket, then off he went to fill them again.

"Slow down, Jeremiah," his mama chided with a laugh. "You gonna wear yo mama out pickin' so fas'."

His mama, Lythia, once served as a housemaid

in Logantree's Big House, but she preferred working in the fields where she could be near her son. Also, she reflected bitterly, in the fields she escaped the brutish advances of Massa Logantree.

Not so in her cabin. Time after painful time had she been subjected to Logantree's drunken attacks in the middle of the night. He forced himself upon her, emptying into her agonized body his vile desire.

Jeremiah recalled with pain the day his mother pointed out to him the man who was his father.

Logantree rarely visited the fields, leaving supervision of the laborers to the overseers. On that day, he came to check the progress of the field hands and was enraged by the slowness with which Elihu was filling his cotton basket.

"Lazy lout!" the planter screamed, lashing Elihu's back with a leather whip. Elihu fell to the ground, and wrapped his head in his arms to ward off further blows. Logantree kicked him in the head with a heavy boot and kept kicking him until Elihu didn't move any more. Elihu was dead.

Jeremiah couldn't tear his eyes away from the horrifying scene.

His mother calmly concentrated on her picking. "That yo pappy, Jeremiah," she said. "No need to be proud."

Jeremiah felt no pride of being the offspring of the white plantation owner. He hated the man he could never claim as his father, the man who beat a field hand to death. And the other part—about what Logantree did to his mama—was too painful to look back on. Maybe someday he could think about it when it wouldn't hurt so much, but never without the hatred coming back.

As a young boy, Jeremiah's mama instilled in him a sense of pride of who he was, and what he might someday become. That lesson gave him the courage to deal with the arrogance of people like Simon Bridges. He watched Bridges strut off down the Vicksburg street.

Jeremiah released his hold on the barber pole and fell in a few steps behind.

Bridges went a dozen paces before he sensed he was being followed. He stopped and faced the black man.

Jeremiah pulled up short.

"What are you doing, boy?" Bridges demanded, pointing an accusing finger at Jeremiah's nose. His bushy eyebrows came together in a point above his pitted nose. "Are you following me, boy?"

"Where at is Nicodemus?" Jeremiah asked.

"What's that you say?"

"I hear you say Nicodemus and promise land."

"You been listening in on my conversations, boy?"

"I don't mean no hurt, sir."

"Don't you know it could get you in a heap of trouble?"

"I just want to know where is Nicodemus."

Not wanting to be seen in the company of a former slave, Bridges took a cautious look around. "Well." The agent's tone softened. "Nicodemus is in a place called Kansas." He studied the confused expression on the black man's face. "You know about Kansas?"

Jeremiah's friend Lemuel said something about

Kansas one day in John Bartlett's blacksmith shop, but he had no idea where to find it.

"No, sir," Jeremiah said. "I don't know 'bout Kansas."

"Do you know where you are now?"

"I hear somebody say Vicksburg."

"That's right. Vicksburg, Mississippi."

"Where at is Kansas?"

Bridges took another look around. Satisfied that he wasn't seen by some white friend or official, he took a step closer to the black man. "Kansas is out west."

"Is that where the promise land is?"

"Nicodemus. Some black folks have settled out there. You won't find any white folks in Nicodemus."

Jeremiah gave his head a thoughtful nod. He couldn't imagine what it would be like in a place where there were no white people.

"No white folks," he said, as if to himself.

Simon's eyes were drawn to the brown face and the smooth lips of the man who stood six inches taller than his own six feet. A thirty-seven-year-old freedman, sturdy of body, with bulging biceps near to bursting the sleeves of his brown muslin shirt. Bridges wished he'd had a hundred like this one before the emancipation. Sold at auction, he'd be rich.

"You want to go to Nicodemus?"

Jeremiah searched Mississippi from one end to the other, and top to bottom in a futile quest for his family. Maybe Nicodemus really was the Promised Land. If there were no white folks there, and black folks were going there, he'd go see if LouEtta and the boys were there.

"Yes, sir, I do," he said.

"Have you got twenty dollars?"

Jeremiah shook his head. Never had he seen twenty dollars at one time. Nor did he know the going rate for passage to St. Louis was only four dollars, not twenty.

Bridges was not ready to give up. He couldn't resist trying to extract a few extra dollars from an unsuspecting former slave who wouldn't know the difference. What did he know about money anyway? "Have you got ten dollars?" he said.

Again Jeremiah shook his head.

Bridges scratched his chin whiskers. He frowned with a serious look on his face, as if searching for the solution to a weighty problem. "Well, that's too bad," he said, trying to appear as sad as he sounded. "If you had a little money I might could find a way to get you to Nicodemus."

A former slave driver, Bridges wasn't inclined to charity, but neither did he want to lose this black giant for lack of a few dollars. On the prairies of Kansas he'd be useful for keeping the peace among pilgrims who traveled hundreds of miles to stake their claims in the new Eden.

"What's your name, boy?" Bridges said.

"Jeremiah Higgins."

Bridges reached into a pocket and brought out a white card. "Can you read?" he said.

The law prohibited slaves from reading and writing. Even so, Massa Logantree's wife believed "even slaves have a right to read and do numbers."

She offered to teach anyone who wanted to learn. At LouEtta's urging, Jeremiah attended the secret sessions in Mrs. Logantree's root cellar.

"I can read some," Jeremiah said to Bridges.

Bridges held the card out to him. "This card will tell you where the staging area is. Take it over there and give it to a man named Wilkins. He's making up a boatload of people leaving for St. Louis on their way to Kansas. You tell him Simon Bridges gave you the card, and maybe he can get you on that boat. Do you think you can do that, boy?"

Jeremiah took the card. He couldn't make out all the words, but he told himself this may be his only chance to get to the Promised Land.

"Yes, sir," he said.

"If Wilkins can get you to St. Louis, some people there will help you on out to Kansas. I'll be out there again in a few weeks. When you get to Nicodemus, I want you to look me up. Simon Bridges. Can you remember that?"

"Simon Bridges. Yes, sir."

Bridges started walking away. He stopped and took a long look at the big black man.

"You hungry, boy?"

Jeremiah bristled. He wished he'd stop calling him boy. He was a man, and if he had a mind to do so, he could break Simon Bridges over his knee.

"No, sir." Jeremiah's answer sprang from the pride his mama taught him. "I'm not hungry."

Jeremiah knew well what it was like to be hungry. He remembered the times he ran away from Logantree's plantation because he didn't want to "die slavin'." He was hunted down by men with guns and bloodhounds and brought back in chains. They threw him into a square cage called "the box" with nothing to eat or drink except three biscuits and a cup of water once a day.

You talkin' 'bout hungry? Jeremiah knew about hungry. Big and strong though he was, after a week in the box with nothing but biscuits and water to keep him alive, even he was too weak to run.

The next time he tried to get away, Logantree traded him to a planter in a distant part of Mississippi.

Jeremiah wondered if the big-bellied Bridges was ever hungry.

"When was the last time you had anything to eat?" Bridges said.

The day before yesterday at the Emanuel Baptist Church in Vicksburg a woman named Delilah Withrow gave him some yams and hog fat. He hadn't eaten since, but his mama's pride tied his tongue. He didn't want Bridges to know how bad off he was.

Jeremiah was grateful to Bridges for helping him get to Kansas, and dared not impose on him further. He could live hungry for a while longer.

"I'm not hungry," he said again.

"Uh-huh," Bridges grunted. He'd dealt with men like Jeremiah before, but never had one of them refused food. "You tell Wilkins I said to give you some grub." Again he started walking away, then turned back. "Why do you want to go to Nicodemus?"

"My wife and boys," Jeremiah said.

"You got family out there?"

"I need to go see."

Bridges humphed at that. "As good a reason as any, I guess."

"My wife, LouEtta, and my boys Joseph and Jacob," Jeremiah said.

Bridges stopped statue still. For a long moment he hesitated, ashen faced, like a man trying to decide whether throwing himself over the cliff might be the best thing to do after all. His attitude changed abruptly.

"You got no money," Bridges said gruffly, "I can't help you. Maybe you don't need to go to Kansas anyhow."

Jeremiah watched him stalk away as if there was something he couldn't wait to get done. Had Bridges changed his mind about helping him get to Nicodemus? Does that mean he wouldn't ever get there? He glanced at the card in his hand. Useless now, he thought, and he almost tossed it away. He changed his mind and tucked the card in a pocket.

With the help of a few inquiries, Jeremiah found the staging area. Never had he seen so many people in one place. Swarms of black faces flooded the dock. Many of them were there for hours, some overnight, waiting. They were tired, impatient, or angry because so many times boarding had been delayed.

Jeremiah found Wilkins standing on a bale of cotton, waving his arms, shouting to the impatient gathering. Wilkins tried to soothe their anger by explaining that the ship's captain suddenly fell ill, and his replacement hadn't yet arrived. Amid groans of disbelief, Wilkins jumped off the bale and stomped away.

Jeremiah was able to get close enough to show Wilkins the card Bridges gave him.

"Mr. Bridges, he say--"

Wilkins snatched the card away, took a brief look, and stomped away without a word. When he came back, he told Jeremiah he found a place for him on the boat to St. Louis.

Jeremiah nodded, and breathed a sigh of relief.

Finally aboard the steamer "Joe Kinney", Jeremiah tried to believe he was really sailing up the Mississippi River without having to ask anybody if it was all right.

He stepped aside as fellow passengers pressed past with arms, backs and shoulders laden with trunks, suitcases, and bed rolls tied around the middle with cotton cords. Women with babies lodged on their hips gripped the hands of older children. Most carried bags or boxes of food for the eight-day trip to St. Louis, where there would be "food aplenty for one and all".

Jeremiah brought with him nothing but what he wore on his back, along with the driving determination to find his wife and babies. Of course, they weren't babies any more. When he last saw them Jacob was two, and Joseph was going on one. Now they would be–what?–fifteen and fourteen? My, my! Could it have been that long? Jeremiah fretted that his sons might not recognize him. But LouEtta would know him.

He would never forget the terror in her eyes the day Logantree traded him away.

Slaves were denied the common courtesies white

people took for granted. He wasn't even allowed to tell his frantic family goodbye. Slaves were considered property, like cattle and horses whose owners could do with them whatever they wanted.

They didn't ask Jeremiah if he wanted to be traded to a faraway planter. He left behind a heartbroken wife and two babies too young to understand why their daddy was torn from them. Nor did anyone ask LouEtta if it was all right if they dragged her husband away, a father who would never again hold his sons, who couldn't comfort them with a gentle pat when they cried out in the night.

The overseers locked chains around his ankles, tied him in the wagon, and hauled him away like a bale of cotton.

Jeremiah looked back, struggling to keep from crying out when he saw the tears streaming down LouEtta's face. She bundled her wailing babies in her arms, and ran after the wagon until she was too exhausted to run any more. She dropped to her knees and prayed for a miracle, for God to stop what was happening to her family.

The miracle never came. Jeremiah couldn't even tell LouEtta not to worry, that they would be together again someday. They both knew they probably would not.

Consternation blanketed the Southland like fear of the plague when, in1862, the U. S. Congress passed the controversial Homestead Act that motivated black people to desert the plantations and seek land of their own. As a result, the planters found themselves having to produce crops without the help of the Negroes. For generations, slaves performed the tasks landowners were not obliged to do, but now found themselves compelled to plant and harvest.

Jeremiah Higgins spent much of his life sweating at the end of a hoe handle. He knew nothing of the Homestead Act until after the war made him a "free man". Nor did he know that another act of Congress, the Thirteenth Amendment to the Constitution, passed in 1865, officially sounded the death knell of slavery.

Furthermore, the Fourteenth Amendment of 1868 granted former slaves the right to citizenship. And in 1870, the Fifteenth Amendment banished all control of landowners over black people, prohibiting any abridgment to voting rights based on "color, race, or previous condition of servitude".

Except for "Mr. Lincoln's paper" that released him from the ownership of his master, Jeremiah was privy to none of these revolutionary developments designed to secure his freedom from slavery. His first knowledge of "free land" had come from his friend Lemuel, and Jeremiah scoffed at that.

"Ain't nobody givin' us nothin'," he said to Lemuel.

# CHAPTER FIVE

Though Jeremiah knew nothing of the Homestead Act, Hill had recognized the rewards of exploiting the former slaves under the umbrella of legitimacy the act provided. He needed help to accomplish his mission. For that purpose, he sought men like Simon Bridges.

Before he was commissioned by Hill to encourage the ex-slaves to move there, Bridges never heard of Kansas. He was a plantation overseer. His experience dealing with slaves prompted Hill to engage him as an agent.

Bridges was eager to capitalize on the dreams of the freedmen. He joined the campaign to persuade the Negroes, who had nothing, to risk their lives for something. He painted life on the prairie of northwest Kansas in glowing terms of joy and happiness and freedom from the drudgery of their previous life.

Shouts of elation might have been heard as far away as Jackson when the gangplank was raised and the hawsers slipped free. The wait was over. The boat whistle blared, and the "Joe Kinney" churned away from the dock. The murky waters of the Mississippi River lapped at its hull, and the journey from Vicksburg to St. Louis was underway.

Jeremiah scanned the faces of the milling crowd, hoping to find one that looked like LouEtta. Oh, he'd know her all right. All those years hadn't erased the image of her soft eyes and smiling lips. Maybe he'd find her in St. Louis. If not there, surely she'd be waiting for him in the magical place called Kansas.

His thoughts mingled with the ship's widening wake when he felt someone elbowing in beside him at the rail. It was a young brown-skinned woman with big round eyes and a smile about two hands wide.

"So, you Big Boy, huh?" she said.

"No."

"That man back there call you Big Boy."

"That ain't my name."

"What is yo name?"

Jeremiah was not eager to engage in idle conversation with this strange lady, but he supposed her question deserved an answer.

"Jeremiah," he said.

"Huh. I like Big Boy better." She wriggled in between him and the ship's rail, and looked squarely into his face. "Where you goin'?"

"They told me St. Louis."

"I know St. Louis. That's where everybody go. I

mean after that."

"Kansas."

"Uh-huh. You ever been to Kansas?"

"No, ma'am."

"Don't call me ma'am. That's what they call my mama 'fore she died."

Jeremiah rolled that over in his mind a time or two, recalling the agony of having been forced to watch his mama die.

"Yo mama die?" he said.

"Everybody's mama die. No room in this world for live mamas."

He turned his attention back to the river and wished she'd go away.

"You married, Big Boy?" She was still there.

"I was."

"You was. That mean you ain't now?"

He couldn't think of an answer that would satisfy her.

"I tell you what, Big Boy, if I ever seen a man 'at needed to be married, it's you." She grabbed his chin and yanked it around. "You got the saddest eyes I ever seen on a man. Looks to me like you in bad need of somebody to take care of you, Big Boy." She stuck out her hand and grabbed his in a brief shake. "Rachel Butterfield. I am mighty proud to make yo acquaintance."

Jeremiah shifted uncomfortably.

"You looked like you was about to bust out bawling," Rachel said, "and I couldn't stand that."

A few more minutes of chatter were all Rachel had time for, but before she left, she coaxed a small smile from the lips of Jeremiah Higgins. She assured him he hadn't seen the last of Rachel Butterfield.

Nice lady, he conceded, but his thoughts were elsewhere.

The waters of the Mississippi grew stronger and wider, sweeping south from its trickling origin in Minnesota to the Gulf of Mexico. For untold ages it carried the canoes of Indian tribes who respected the size and might of what they called the Great River. Pioneers had challenged its waters, rampaging one minute, calm as flowing molasses the next. Whatever its mood, the river rumbled unchecked to the fertile valleys dotted with homesteads. Its restless waters plied by paddle-wheeled steamboats brought goods to towns and villages clinging to its banks.

"Here come de boat!" was the rallying cry for festive occasions for blacks and whites alike.

Along its 2350-mile serpentine journey, the Mississippi's banks were lined with cities, plantations, and villages, where dwellers in mansions and shanties alike respected its waters as a living being.

From the ship's rail, Jeremiah marveled at the tumbling waters. They stirred in him a strange and wonderful excitement by which explorers and pioneers he never heard of hundreds of years before must have been stricken.

As the "Joe Kinney" knifed its way through the churning waters, Jeremiah wondered what lay ahead in St. Louis. But, what lay behind brought him back, as it always did, to LouEtta and the boys.

After Logantree traded him away to a strange

planter, Jeremiah lay awake on a straw pallet night after lonely night, looking back, aching for his family, wondering if he would ever see them again.

Their last night together, LouEtta had wriggled out from under him and soon was asleep.

On the pallet beside their bed, the boys had long since dropped off.

Jeremiah couldn't sleep. He lay awake thinking. Jacob and Joseph were born into slavery with no hope of anything better. Condemned to a life of drudgery, until their bodies were bent and used up long before they were supposed to be. One day they'd be sold or traded and suffer the horror of being separated from their families. Many times he'd seen it happen. The thought of his sons being subjected to such sorrow shot daggers of pain through his heart.

Jeremiah wept. He covered his trembling lips with a calloused hand to keep his sobs from waking LouEtta.

She stirred beside him. "You awake, Jeremiah?"

He didn't answer.

"What you thinkin' 'bout?" she said.

"Nothin'. I ain't thinking 'bout nothin'."

"You better be thinkin' 'bout somethin'–like gettin' some sleep. Massa don't like nigger boys sleepin' on they's hoe han'les in the fiel'."

Jeremiah took a moment to think about that. "I can't do it, LouEtta."

"What yo can't do?"

"I can't let my boys die slavin'."

"Uh-huh. And what you gonna do, black boy? You gonna buy this plantation and cut all us colored folks loose?"

LouEtta adored Jeremiah. She shared his dream of "bustin' loose" and making a better life for his family, but long since she lost hope that the dream would ever come true. She'd seen too many hard times, too many slaves beaten and bleeding, sold off or traded after they tried to escape.

Three times she agonized over Jeremiah when the night riders dragged him back in chains. She suffered with him when they threw him in the box-- not big enough for him to stretch his long legs. No food nor drink, except for the scant three biscuits and a cup of water that wouldn't keep a small child alive. Once, she brought him food, and was beaten for trying to give it to him. She watched the overseer throw it to the dogs.

LouEtta knew no punishment could break Jeremiah's spirit. He'd never give up. He wouldn't quit trying, no matter how loudly the bloodhounds bayed in pursuit, nor how savagely they nipped at his heels. He would try again. One day, he told himself, he'd make it, and it would be worth all the beatings and going without food.

In the small cabin's darkness LouEtta couldn't see the smile creasing Jeremiah's face. "Maybe," he said.

"What maybe?"

"Maybe I just walk right up to the Big House and knock on the door and say, 'Massa, I come into a lot of money, and I think I just buy yo plantation so's I can let all the black folks go.' What you think of that?"

"I think you crazy, Jeremiah," LouEtta said, but

a chuckle crept into her voice. "You better be putting your thinkin' where it'll do some good." She turned over and went back to sleep.

When daylight came, Jeremiah was still awake. Thinking.

Before the sun was noon high the next day, LouEtta watched, horrified, as they hauled Jeremiah away.

A gunny sack wouldn't hold all the reasons why the freedmen fled the South. One was a group of white supremacists who called themselves the Ku Klux Klan. Formed in 1866 as a social group for veterans, the Klan soon became recognized as "The Invisible Empire of the South." Klan members wrapped themselves in bed sheets, hid their faces with hoods to avoid being identified.

The Klan stalked the blacks like hungry hounds. They ravaged their homes, planted burning crosses in their yards. They often left black men hanging by the neck from tree limbs in their own yards in front of their agonized wives and children.

Defeat of the Confederacy ended slavery, but the former slaves were haunted yet by the threat of lynching by the Klan. Planters hired thugs to terrorize them, threatening any who might leave the plantations.

The plight of the freedmen changed little from what they suffered before the war, and clouds of oppression still hovered long after the last shot was fired.

Legal statutes kept their movements under strict surveillance, humiliated by decrees of the past, such as Alabama's 1862 code which charged patrols to "...enter by force if necessary all Negro cabins or quarters, kitchens, and out houses, and apprehend all slaves found there not belonging to the plantation household without a pass from their owner or overseer, or strolling from place to place without authority."

For more than two hundred years a planter's "inherent right" to buy, sell, or trade a slave was sanctioned by the states. Slave patrols were authorized to arrest and punish anyone whose face was not white. If a slave ran away, he was hunted down by bulldozers with guns and clubs and snarling bloodhounds. He was dragged back, shackled hand and foot, his neck burned raw by a hempen noose.

In Louisiana's Avoyelles Parish, patrols were empowered to "take and punish slaves found away from their masters' premises without a permit." Some were seized by mobs to prevent their migrating to Kansas. Blood-chilling accounts of violence, such as the lynching of two former slaves in Vicksburg, warned of what could happen to any black who deserted the plantation.

State laws were designed to benefit the landowners. Though the planters couldn't work the fields without them, most had little respect for blacks as human beings. When President Lincoln was assassinated after the war ended in 1865, Vice President Andrew Johnson moved into the White House. One of his first official acts was to veto a civil rights bill that declared, "Blacks are not ready for the privileges nor equality of citizens." Indeed, the Democrats' political platform stated, "...we hold this to be a government of white people, made and perpetuated for the exclusive benefit of the white race. People of African descent cannot be considered citizens of the United States, and there can, in no event, nor under any circumstances, be any equality between the white and black races."

Such proclamations fed the flames of resentment among the freedmen, strengthening their resolve to escape the humiliation of life on the plantations, beyond whose borders lay their hope for the future. No longer did they want to cultivate the land of their white masters, laboring in the fields from sun up until darkness drove them in. They longed for land of their own, to plant corn, beans, and potatoes, and claim for themselves the fruits of their labor.

So it was, when news of a "promised land" called Nicodemus swept the Southland, droves of former slaves packed up their meager belongings and headed west. What they would find in Kansas they didn't know–but, driven by dreams of freedom from the white man's rule, they couldn't wait to get there.

Jeremiah, though eager to escape the brutality of the Klan and night riders, didn't look beyond the hope of finding his family. The boat ride to St. Louis, therefore, was only a step toward that end.

"So, there you are, Big Boy!" Rachel's arrival brought sunshine into shadowy corners, and the sound of her voice made Jeremiah smile. "I been lookin' all over for you," she said.

"I'm here," he said. "Not much place else to go."

Rachel wriggled in beside him at the ship's rail.

For a while they watched in silence as the river rolled by. She waved to people along the river banks, and they waved back. Most of them likely wished they could go too. Where didn't matter.

"Yo mama die?" Rachel said.

Jeremiah was startled by the question. He didn't want to talk about his mother's death. It was still too vivid, too painful to think back on. "She die."

Even now, all those years later, his ears ached with the sound of his mama's horrified screams on that night he was jarred awake by her pitiful cries, struggling to free herself from another ravaging attack by the boorish Logantree.

Jeremiah hovered in a corner of the small cabin, crying eye-burning tears, watching helplessly, trying not to watch Logantree's assault on his mama. Once, he leaped on the back of the landowner, trying to make him stop the brutal attack.

Logantree shoved him against the cabin wall.

His mama screamed and Logantree hit her. She screamed again and he hit her harder. She fought back, flailing away with both fists against his chest. Logantree cursed her and battered her face and stomach, and choked her until she didn't fight any more. .

Jeremiah was eight years old. His mama was dead.

Only LouEtta heard Jeremiah talk about what happened that tragic night.

But now, along came this strange, vibrant, brown-skinned lady who befriended him, this woman who said her name was Rachel Butterfield.

She asked if his mama died, and he told her.

Rachel understood. She had witnessed the death of her own mother in a struggle with a white overseer. She shared Jeremiah's pain. She cried.

To support the search for his family, along the way Jeremiah traded the skills he learned from Aaron. One such pause was at the Bartlett farm in western Mississippi. Young John Bartlett learned early that Jeremiah Higgins, a former slave, was a man to be reckoned with.

Rolling in sweat from brow to belt, Jeremiah stoked the forge in Bartlett's blacksmith shop. His friend Lemuel plopped down on a nearby stump. Jeremiah's nod acknowledged Lem's arrival. He kept swinging the hammer, pounding a piece of red hot metal.

Lemuel was a slender man of forty. A round straw hat was plopped on his head. He spat a stream of tobacco juice. A mischievous smile sneaked across his face between his scraggly chin whiskers and mustache. Anxious to share news he thought Jeremiah would be excited to hear, Lemuel's eyes sparkled with anticipation.

"Know what I hear?" Lem said that day in Bartlett's blacksmith shop.

Jeremiah tossed his hammer aside and breathed a deep sigh. "What you hear, Lem?"

"Grapevine say some folks talkin' 'bout a new promise lan'."

Jeremiah's chest glistened with sweat. With a dubious shake of his head, he grabbed the tongs and went back to work. In the bed of coals he buried the metal till it glowed red, hot enough to pound into a plow share. He dragged an already sweat-soaked rag from his hip pocket and mopped his brow.

"A new promise lan'?" he said to Lem. "Ain't seen the old one yet."

Lemuel chuckled at that. "They say somers out west. Place called Kansas. They say a man can get hisself a piece o' gov'ment ground for next to nothin'."

"They say, they say," Jeremiah chided. "Who say?"

"Grapevine say a man name of Pap Singleton over to Jackson. He say."

"He been there?"

"Don't know. Nobody been there and back, I heard of," Lem said.

"Nobody been to hell and back either."

"What you told me, it sound like you have," Lem said.

"Maybe," Jeremiah said with a nod. "Who is Pap Singleton?"

"He one of us. They say he tryin' to help us find a way."

Jeremiah scoffed at that. "Ain't no nigger got money for lan'."

"Uh-huh, I hear you."

"You goin'?"

Lemuel shook his head no. "Who me? No. I got roots here."

"Roots." Jeremiah thought about that for a moment. "Better off here likely. Gov'ment ain't doin' nothin' for us. We just a bunch o' poor black niggers that ain't got nothin', never had nothin', and never will have nothin'."

Lemuel brought a folded piece of yellow paper from a pocket and waved it at Jeremiah. "You read?"

"If I need to."

Lemuel unfolded the paper and handed it to him.

Jeremiah studied the paper for a moment. He began reading aloud, struggling with some of the words. "Free lan'. Free hoss and plow. Free seeds." He skipped to the bottom of the flier. "Plezmore Shippin' Comp'ny, Vicksburg." He handed the paper back to Lemuel. "Ain't nothin' but trash, Lem. Ain't nobody gon be givin' us nothin'."

"No lie."

Jeremiah heard the gravelly voice of John Bartlett. Jeremiah was surprised to see him leaning against a post, puffing on a cigar.

Bartlett was a hollow-chested thirty-three-year-old man of medium build who inherited his father's cotton farm. He felt no attachment to the soil, except for the money it provided for his addiction to gambling aboard the riverboats. Like many of the Southern aristocracy, Bartlett nurtured the notion that Lee's surrender only ended the bloodshed, not the war.

He paid a man to march off and fight in his place, and had no doubt the South would rise again. The war was long ago over, but Bartlett still viewed the black man as a slave whose only reason for living was to do the bidding of his white master. He puffed on the cigar and blew out a fog of gray smoke that hid his sallow face. When the smoke cleared, he said to Jeremiah, "There's some blacks leaving, but you won't be one of them." To Lemuel, he said, "What're you doing here, boy?"

Lem fidgeted, wishing he were someplace else.

"Lem come to see me," Jeremiah said. "He ain't no hurt."

"It looks to me like he's making you drag your feet," Bartlett said. "You don't go any place till I say you can."

Jeremiah cast a glance at Lemuel.

Lem's eyes got wide with fright, still wary of the white man's voice.

"I'll think about that," Jeremiah said.

"No thinking to it," Bartlett said. "You try leaving here before you get that job done and I'll have the dogs on your tail before you make a track."

Jeremiah took up the tongs, clamped them around the red hot metal, and lifted it chest high between himself and the sneering Bartlett.

"Mr. Bartlett," he said, "the war was over a long time ago. Mr. Lincoln say I'm a free man, and Mr. Grant back him up. That mean I can go anyplace I want, any time I want to. Now, sir, are you tellin' me I can't go 'way from here if I'm a mind to?"

Bartlett stared at the big man hoisting the metal within inches of his face, trying to decide whether Jeremiah use it on him. "Are you threatening me, boy?" he said.

"Just askin'."

Bartlett abhorred the thought of being bested by a former slave, but he hated more the prospect of being scarred for the rest of his life by a piece of red hot metal. "I'll have your wages tomorrow morning," he said.

"Thank you, sir."

When morning came, Jeremiah collected his wages and thought about what to do next. Lem's paper said the Plezmore outfit was in Vicksburg. He turned his eyes that way and started walking. He didn't know yet that he'd be boarding the steamer "Joe Kinney" at Vicksburg for a trip up the Mississippi River.

# CHAPTER SIX

St. Louis didn't want them. The levee along the Mississippi was already swarming with former slaves in makeshift huts and shanties. They hovered around campfires, warming themselves against the early spring chill.

The city fathers worked themselves into a dither trying to find ways to cope with the masses of Negroes the boats kept dumping on them. City officials threatened to sue the steamboat companies if they brought more. The shippers countered that they were "in the cargo business, and anyone who has money for the fare is entitled to ride".

St. Louis was not alone in its frustration. The Southern planters were up in arms, condemning the exodus of former slaves. They decried the loss of cheap labor they depended on for tending the crops, and protested that slave holding was their inherent right. Why the blacks wanted to leave the plantations was far beyond the planters' comprehension. Were they not fed and clothed as well as they could expect to be? The landowner's mindset was, he was born to be served, with no appreciation for the plight of the slaves. The prospect of facing life without them was an unthinkable reality.

From New Orleans to New York, the planters' cause was championed by newspaper editors, disparaging the "outlandish promises of land promoters" from the West. Some called people like Simon Bridges "railroad agents," lackeys of the rail lines whose property along the tracks they hoped to sell "at unscrupulous prices" to unsuspecting migrants. Furthermore, the blacks were portrayed as "indolent and shiftless". If left alone to provide for themselves, the press proclaimed, they were "doomed to failure".

Such editorials were designed to bolster the cause of the plantation owners whose cotton, rice, tobacco, indigo and sugar cane were the lifeblood of the South. Without slave labor, they were helpless to produce those crops.

The editors' campaign, admonishing the blacks to return to the only way of life they knew was blunted by most blacks' inability to read. Those who "could read some" were not dissuaded from their determination to separate themselves from the drudgery of life on the plantations.

And so it was that Jeremiah Higgins joined the throng of freedmen, powerless to do anything, except wait for the disgruntled St. Louis city officials to find a way to deal with them. Jeremiah didn't know what the fuss was all about, but he wished they'd get it done, so he could resume his journey to the "John Brown country" called Kansas.

Jeremiah didn't know much about John Brown, except that Brown and his sons waged a personal battle against slavery and led an attack on the Federal arsenal at Harper's Ferry, Virginia. Brown's goal was to capture arms and ammunition to expand his personal war against slavery.

A few years before, Brown moved to Kansas from New England. When pro-slavery forces sacked the free-state town of Lawrence, Brown and his five sons countered by killing five of the pros along Pottawattamie Creek.

Brown's disastrous attack at Harper's Ferry that spelled the end for Brown and his company of twenty-two followers, ten of whom were Negroes. Not one escaped, and those who survived the battle were hanged. One of the survivors was John Brown. Charged with treason, Brown was found guilty, sentenced to death by hanging.

Even so, millions of slaves prayed for something to hope for. In the fields and around campfires, the name of John Brown was uttered with reverence. Brown alone waged open warfare against the evils of slavery. Even in failure, he was exalted by the beleaguered blacks as a hero who championed their cause. Joining the exodus from the South, they marched to the tune of "John Brown's body lies a-moldering in the grave".

Still, their hearts remained full of hope and anticipation of new beginnings in a place called

Nicodemus, where there were no slaves and no white masters. They put their trust in God to provide the ground to which they could attach their names, and proclaim, "This is mine!"

St. Louis Mayor John Overholtz was opposed to the exodus of slaves from the South and was accused by his Republican colleagues of being a Democrat. The accusation so rankled the mayor that he broke out in hives. He defended his position as "not opposed to providing shelter for the freedmen, as long as there are not too many of them". He never defined how many would be "too many". He feared "if we give too much to too many, the city of St. Louis would become a refuge for fleeing indigents".

Not only did Overholtz not want to encourage the continued migration of emancipated slaves to his city, he also was faced with the dilemma of what to do with those already there.

While the city fathers fiddled, the restless blacks along the banks of the Mississippi stewed in juices of uncertainty. They milled around the levees, pooling their bewilderment, and speculated on what was going to become of them. They huddled around campfires, traded guesses, and tried without success to make sense of rampant rumors.

One story making the rounds was that they were going to be shipped out to a place called Wyandotte, Kansas. That sparked debate as to whether Wyandotte was near Nicodemus, and if it was not, why were they going there?

"It don't bother me none," Jeremiah said in a

conversation with himself. He set his fire apart to separate himself from a handful of rowdies who, bored with nothing better to do, spent time intimidating the weary campers.

"As long as it's Kansas," Jeremiah reasoned, "that's fine with me. Nicodemus got to be out there some place."

He hadn't seen Rachel for a while, but he spent little time wondering why. Though he enjoyed her visits, he made no effort to encourage it. She'd popped up unexpectedly before, and she likely would pop up again.

Out of the corner of his eye Jeremiah caught sight of the slouching approach of two black men—a couple of the bullies he'd seen pushing and shoving their neighbors with brash talk. They were looking for ways to relieve the frustration of waiting to find out what was going to happen to them. It didn't matter who they picked on, but Jeremiah, alone at his fire, they pegged as an easy mark.

Times when Jeremiah ran away from Logantree's plantation, it took four men to bring him down. Even so, watching the troublemakers approach, he was smart enough to know at thirty-seven he was not as strong as he was back then. He could tell by the look on their faces these men were up to no good. Before it was over, somebody would get hurt, and he wasn't ready for it to be him.

"What say, Big Boy?" one of the men said with a grin. A heavy set man with a knife scar on his left cheek, he knelt on one knee, and talked to Jeremiah across the fire. His friend knelt beside him.

"How come you way off over here all by

yo'self?" Scarface wanted to know.

Squatted on his heels, Jeremiah shook his head. No use trying to explain anything to this no-good. "I don't mix much," he said.

"Lookee here," said the first man, jabbing his friend in the ribs. "Big Boy say he don't mix much." The two laughed at that.

Two other men joined the circle.

"Go on by," Jeremiah said.

The four laughed as if Jeremiah had told a funny story.

"Big Boy say go on by," the scar-faced one said. To Jeremiah, he said, "That mean you better'n us?"

"No. I ain't better'n nobody."

"How come you camped 'way off over here?"

"I got my own fire," Jeremiah said.

Jeremiah's eyes swept the circle of black faces staring at him. He knew what they were up to. Restless from helping each other fret over when the white man was going to decide what to do with them, they were looking for something to do to break the monotony of what they were doing already.

Jeremiah was in the middle of working out how he'd defend himself when the fight started. He found out when two of the ruffians grabbed his arms, a third leaped on his back, and the fourth man pounded his stomach. With a mighty swing of his arms, Jeremiah discovered that his strength had not deserted him. He flung aside the two bullies clinging to his arms. The man pummeling his mid-section got a knee in the face that sent him sprawling. Jeremiah grabbed the fourth roughneck by the collar and launched him over his head onto the gravel. The man staggered to his feet, and limped away, holding his head in his hands.

Jeremiah thought the fray was over, but a blow to the back of his head knocked him to the ground. He didn't get up.

How long Jeremiah lay there he didn't know. When he woke up, the first voice he heard was Rachel Butterfield's.

"Big Boy!" She fussed over him. "What them niggers do to you?"

"I'm all right."

"You don't look all right to me. Hold still while I clean yo face."

He shook his head clear. From somewhere he heard a man's voice pleading for attention.

"Please, hear me," the voice said, loud and clear.

In the light of a bonfire across the way, Jeremiah saw a slender black man standing on top of a bale of cotton. He waved his arms and spread his hands for quiet. "My name is Charlton Tandy," Jeremiah heard him say.

Jeremiah never heard of Charlton Tandy, but Tandy sounded different from the others who came to tell the refugees what they needed to do.

Tandy's speech was cultured, his grammar flawless. "Like you," he said, "I was once a slave. I know what you're up against, and I understand what you're going through."

Anyone who didn't talk like they talked wasn't to be trusted. Tandy's comments were greeted with derisive titters, along with a few pointed suggestions disparaging his ancestry.

"Amen, brother!" the skeptics chided. "You betcha, Mr. Tandy."

But Tandy would not be put off. "I know," he said, gesturing for calm. "It's not easy. But there are people here in St. Louis who want to help you."

As he spoke, the listeners sidled closer, grumbling about another "speechifier". But they listened for lack of anything better to do. At least this one, they conceded, sounded like he knew what he was talking about.

"You going over there?" Rachel said.

"No," Jeremiah said. "I stay here and mind the fire."

She dropped to her knees beside him. "Me too."

"It don't take two to mind the fire."

"I'm stayin'."

While city officials languished in a hotbed of apathy, Tandy negotiated with some churches and social agencies, seeking help for the bewildered refugees. Women's groups from the churches set up soup lines on the levees and provided warm clothing and blankets for the children against the dampness.

"I know you're cold and hungry," Tandy said. "I share your frustration, but everything takes time." He explained that the authorities encountered some legal and political obstacles in connection with the freedmen's predicament. "As soon as I can find out what's going on, I'll be back and tell you about it."

The former slaves had been assured they'd be welcome in St. Louis, with accommodations for their well-being. They also were told arrangements would be made for their transfer farther west. Arriving in St. Louis, they were disappointed to find they were misled.

"Lied to!" some protested.

Except for the efforts of Charlton Tandy, the shivering blacks in the makeshift camps were ignored. They agonized over the inactivity of city officials who spent less time looking for ways to relieve their discomfort than on how to get rid of them. Many were forced to swallow their pride. Some ventured beyond the camps, even going door-to-door in the city seeking food for their hungry children.

Answers didn't come easy, but Tandy promised he'd find them.

Tempers flared, and threats of lawsuits and political ostracism vied for time and space in the smoke-filled chamber as the city fathers argued in emergency session. Hours of wrangling and heated debate led only to further wrangling and debate. In the end, it was the mayor himself who threw up his hands in frustration. "If they want to go to Kansas," he shouted, "let's send them the hell to Kansas!"

Tandy attended the meeting on behalf of the refugees and was dispatched to carry the news to the campers on the levees: Each of the freed slaves would receive two dollars for passage by boat, train, pack mule, or by whatever means would most rapidly convey the masses of blacks beyond the limits of the city of St. Louis.

# CHAPTER SEVEN

Smoke boiled from the stack of the steamboat "E. H. Durfee". The hawsers were cast off, and the boat slipped away from the St. Louis dock, bound for Wyandotte, Kansas. Jubilation rose to a deafening level as the Durfee's paddlewheel churned the murky waters of the mighty Missouri River headed west. The steamer's harsh whistle blast was all but drowned out by its black cargo's gleeful shouts and light-hearted singing.

Once again Jeremiah found himself at the ship's rail, peering into the tumbling waters, pondering what lay ahead in Wyandotte. He searched the new river for answers he had not found in the other one.

To the rhythm of waves brushing the hull of the "E. H. Durfee", Jeremiah's memory slipped back again to the plantation where he grew to be a man, where he felt the sting of the lacerating lash and lost his family because of his obsession for freedom--

and where his mother died at the hands of the ruthless Master Logantree.

He recalled the times he stood at a distance, gazing at Logantree's Big House, wondering what it would be like to see inside. That dream fueled his need to escape the degradation of being locked outside. Being chased down and hauled back only challenged his determination to try again.

Jeremiah never realized his dream of seeing behind the walls of the Big House, but LouEtta once served as Mrs. Logantree's handmaiden. He could still see the wonder in LouEtta's eyes as she described the winding oak stairway leading to the floors above the kitchen level: The family's private living quarters; the master's office with its book-lined walls; the huge ballroom on the third floor designed for lavish entertaining. On festive occasions, such as weddings, anniversaries, and harvest time celebrations, friends and neighbors from miles around came to dine and dance at the Big House, often till dawn.

Music and laughter wafted over to the slave quarters, where eager ears listened with longing, wondering if they would ever know such joy.

Beyond the sweet scented magnolias and honeysuckle vines, back of the Big House sprawled the rough-hewn log cabins, home to the cooks, house servants, seamstresses, parlor maids and laundresses. There, too, were the cabins of the carpenters, smithies, leather workers and field hands.

After a day of labor, which began before sunrise and ended after dark, a huge black kettle simmered over an open fire in a large clearing surrounded by the cabins. Jeremiah recalled his mama taking her turn, stirring in spices, adding okra, tomatoes, onions, and hog fat until the taste was just right. When she signaled for bowls and cups to be ladled full of the steaming soup, they all settled into a circle around the fire.

Once the bowls and cups were fingered clean, the circle came alive with music and song.

Jeremiah remembered listening for Miss Julia's haunting contralto. It was hardly more than a whisper at first, rising to a crescendo, like the waves lashing the hull of the Durfee, followed by hand-clapping and foot-stomping.

Sad or happy, the ringing banjo and the twang of the fiddle sounded the same. Words of the songs changed to fit the mood, but the entreaties rarely did. There were pleas to the Lord to "lead us over Jordan", seeking deliverance from the drudgery of life on the plantations.

Jeremiah was brought back by the sounds of joy aboard the steamer Durfee, echoing along the banks of the Missouri River. The sea of black faces glistened with hope as old tunes with new words rose from the throats of the Kansas-bound refugees: "Lord, if there is a Nicodemus, lead me home!"

For Jeremiah, the relief of finally being on his way to Kansas shared space in his thoughts with the sadness of having lost his mother. The pages of memory fluttered back to the night she died by the hand of the drunken Logantree.

Many times Jeremiah fought the urge to go back to whatever was left of the Logantree plantation.

Not to fulfill his dream of viewing inside the Big House, but in his mind he could see himself coming face-to-face with his former master, seeking revenge for his mother's death.

"You say you're Jeremiah?" he could almost hear Logantree sneer.

"Yes, sir."

"Why have you come back here, boy?"

"I come to kill you," Jeremiah would say.

"Kill me?" The planter's derisive laugh crinkled the hair on Jeremiah's neck. "Why do you want to kill me?"

"Because you killed my mama."

"Your mama? Your mama? Who--who was your mama?"

Slimy bastard! He didn't even remember the name of the woman he raped before he beat her to death!

One day, in his wanderings in search for his family, Jeremiah found himself near Logantree's plantation. He struggled with himself, trying to decide whether to carry out his urge to seek revenge against the brutal landowner. Maybe Logantree was no longer alive. Maybe the war didn't leave enough of his plantation to bother with. He made excuses for not doing what he promised himself he would do given the opportunity.

"I may never be this close again," he reasoned with himself. Finally he yielded to the temptation that gnawed at him since he was eight years old. He made his way along the tree-lined way leading to the Big House he remembered but never saw inside. The intoxicating aroma of magnolias in bloom that filled the air brought him back. Reviving the pain. Trying not to remember, driven by something that would not let him forget.

He drew close enough to see an old man slumped in a wicker chair on the veranda, sunning himself on an autumn afternoon. A plaid blanket covered the old man's lap. His chin rested on his chest, eyes closed, spittle drooled from the corners of his mouth. Even the long white scraggly hair and emaciated body could not hide his identity. Into his purple lips a middle-aged black woman in a white smock spooned what Jeremiah supposed was liquid nourishment.

"That yo pappy, Jeremiah," his mama told him that day in the field. "No need to feel proud."

Never, until now, did Jeremiah concede, even to himself, that Logantree was his father. His mama said he was, and she knew. But Jeremiah couldn't accept the reality of being the son of such a cruel man. He convinced himself he could never claim to be the son of the man who killed his mother.

From his lips escaped the whispered word "father," just to hear what it sounded like, find out how it felt to say it out loud. He'd lived with the revulsion of how it felt, but saying it out loud made it worse. Never had he allowed himself to utter that word. He said it now, not to a dying man, but in pity for the man he came to kill.

Watching the frail old man whose strength rested in the hands of those who served him, Jeremiah felt melting away the vengefulness that compelled him to come. What satisfaction, he argued with himself, would there be in taking the life of a helpless old man who wasn't worth killing and who was near death already?

Jeremiah turned his back on the pathetic scene and walked away.

# CHAPTER EIGHT

Wyandotte didn't want them either. Anticipation of good things for the refugees sank into a dilemma of waiting and frustration. Different people in a different place wrestled with their fate. Wyandotte's business people were not pleased with their city's being selected as a stopover for migrants on their way west. They formed a negotiating committee of leading citizens, and sent them off to persuade St. Louis officials to divert future refugees to some place other than Wyandotte.

"How about Jefferson City, or Independence?" the committee grumbled. "And Kansas City is much better equipped than we to handle such an influx of indigents we don't need and don't want."

Their pleadings fell on deaf ears. The blacks were gone from St. Louis, and Mayor Overstolz made it clear his city assumed no responsibility for what happened to them after they left. The St. Louis position was, "We don't want to know."

While the Wyandotte business community stewed over how masses of black refugees adversely affected the city's economy, some local citizens harbored no such fears. Even the Wyandotte Herald, while cautioning against further arrivals of former slaves, ventured a note of compassion in their behalf: "...a large number of colored immigrants from Louisiana, Alabama, Mississippi and Tennessee landed in Kansas. Nearly all of them are penniless, many are sick, and all are objects of sympathy. A public hearing was held in the court room on Tuesday afternoon to take steps for their relief, and to provide against spreading contagious disease."

The following week the Herald published a response from a group of citizens who strongly opposed their coming, and even more loudly protested their staying:

"In the past weeks over a thousand Negroes landed in Wyandotte. None of them have money.....large numbers died, and many are sick. We have reliable information that thousands more are coming. If so, the situation will soon be serious for the deluded, helpless, and ignorant Negroes rushing to Kansas, and a mighty burden will be thrown on our people. We, the enlightened citizens of Wyandotte, Kansas, denounce those who are encouraging these people to come to Kansas as their worst enemies."

Even so, over the objections of local merchants, boats continued to flood Wyandotte with loads of emancipated blacks. The bewildered refugees huddled along the banks of the Kaw River in crude lean-tos made of scavenged boards and scraps of tin. Official Wyandotte, a town of five thousand citizens, was ill prepared to accommodate the sudden surge in population.

But they misjudged the townspeople's compassion for the hapless blacks.

Churches recognized their dismal plight, and set about finding ways to relieve the freedmen's discomfort. Some local blacks, however, themselves former slaves who became citizens of Wyandotte, resented the influx of their own people. Others opened their homes to them.

The Methodist Church sent a horse-drawn flatbed wagon to bring anyone who wanted to bed down in the warmth of the church's basement. Rain-soaked Negroes took advantage of the opportunity, and rushed to climb aboard the wagon. The team was geed into motion, and the wagon creaked away, slushing through mud and water.

Jeremiah's long legs dangled over the side of the flat bed as the wagon slid along the deep-rutted street.

"So this is Kansas," he mused. Surely Nicodemus couldn't be far away.

It was near dark when the wagon pulled up in front of the church, and Jeremiah scrambled off with two dozen other riders. Inside, he got in a line where churchwomen, with friendly smiles behind makeshift tables, ladled hot vegetable soup into wooden bowls. He thanked the lady who filled his bowl, and settled on his haunches against a wall, and balanced the bowl on a knee.

"That you, Big Boy?"

Jeremiah's hand was half way to his mouth with a spoonful of soup when he heard Rachel's voice. He made no attempt to suppress the smile sneaking across his lips.

She squatted on the floor beside him. "I been worried about you."

"No need to be worryin' 'bout me," Jeremiah said.

"I didn't see you on the wagon."

"I was on it."

"You want more soup?" she asked.

"I wouldn't mind."

She took his bowl and strutted away to get it refilled. When she returned, she said, "I heard some people talkin'."

Jeremiah didn't like the concern he heard in her voice. He hoped what she heard was not as serious as the look on her face. "First time you hear people talkin'?"

"They talkin' 'bout burnin' this place down."

"What place?"

"The church house," she said.

"Burnin' the church house down?"

"That's what they say."

"Who say?"

"A woman over by the soup line. She say she hear some men talkin' 'bout burnin' the church house down."

"Black or white?" he asked.

"Black. But there was somethin' 'bout white folks payin' 'em to do it."

"You know who they talkin' 'bout?"

"Same ones jumped you back in St. Louis."

"Uh-huh." He slid a finger around the inside of the soup bowl, rounding up the last morsel. He licked the finger while he thought about what to say next. "You hear a name?" he said.

"No."

"Who was doin' the talkin'?"

Rachel pointed to a heavy-set black woman with a red bandanna tied around her head.

"That's her over there."

"The men–they in the church?"

"She say they camped outside."

Jeremiah stood up and gave his head a thoughtful nod.

Rachel took his empty bowl and spoon.

"You stay 'way from me now," he said.

"What you gonna do, Big Boy?"

"You go on by."

There were more people in the church yard than in the basement. The rain dwindled to a light drizzle. Those huddled around the fires turned their collars up against the drizzle. Others milled aimlessly about.

Jeremiah made the rounds, looking for the leader of the ruffians who attacked him in St. Louis, the one with the knife scar on his left cheek. He found him warming his hands by a fire. Jeremiah squatted on his heels beside him.

"Well, lookee who's here," said the man with the scar. "If it ain't ol' Big Boy!"

"That's ol' Big Boy all right!" another said.

Jeremiah spread his hands to the fire while he worked out in his mind what he was going to say when somebody asked him what he was doing there.

"What you doing here, Big Boy?"

"Friend o' mine hear somebody talkin' 'bout burnin' the church house down," Jeremiah said.

The faces around the fire reflected outrage that anybody would even think of doing such a vile deed.

"I thought," Jeremiah said, "I might need some help takin' care of 'em."

The four hoodlums looked at each other and shook their heads with innocent disbelief. If they had any thought of attacking the big man again they showed no sign of it. They doubtless recalled the pain of twisted arms and bruised heads from their previous encounter with Jeremiah in St. Louis.

"I 'member what happened back there in St. Louie," Jeremiah said.

The four shifted uneasily and traded questioning glances.

"I gonna let that pass," Jeremiah went on, "'cause when I find them ones talkin' 'bout burnin' the church house down, I might need some help. Hear what I'm sayin'?"

"Oh yeah, Big Boy, we hear you," they chorused. "Yes, sir!"

Jeremiah eyed the faces around the circle and stretched to his full six-feet-six.

The four hoodlums appeared anxious for him to be gone.

"I'm gonna go lookin' for 'em," Jeremiah said. "You be here when I get back?"

"Oh, you bet, Big Boy, we be right chere."

Jeremiah made another circle of the churchyard. When he got back to where he left the ruffians, he wasn't surprised to find them gone.

He would learn they didn't go far enough.


Jeremiah's fingers tightened around the throat of eighteen-year-old Master William Logantree. To assert his authority, the planter's son lashed Jeremiah three times across the back with a bull whip. It had happened before, but Jeremiah never defended himself until now. He knew he'd be severely punished for doing so. This time, two years younger and twenty pounds heavier than young Logantree, Jeremiah knew it was time to fight back.

He grabbed the whip and twisted it out of William's hand. In a fury, he flung the whip aside, and wrestled the young master to the ground.

The squirming William was unable to free himself of the incensed Negro's vise-like grip.

"Kill me!" William gasped. Counting death less humiliating than defeat at the hands of a slave, again he screamed, "Kill me!"

Jeremiah was angry enough to snap his neck, but he relaxed his grip, and let William cough his lungs full.

"Why didn't you kill me?" William said, his voice tinged with loathing.

"I couldn't kill you," Jeremiah said calmly.

"Why not?"

"I couldn't kill my own brother."

"Your brother?" William glared in disbelief that a slave would dare claim to be the son of his father.

"Your daddy was my daddy."

Jeremiah woke up drenched with cold sweat. The dream always did that to him. He was glad it was over.

He felt someone stir on the floor beside him. "That you, Rachel?"

"It's me."

"What you doin'?" he said.

"Keepin' you warm."

"I'm warm."

"Then I'm keepin' me warm."

She pulled the blanket up under her chin and snuggled closer.

In the darkness Jeremiah smiled, rolled over--and smelled smoke. Two sniffs told him the acrid odor was not coming from the pot-bellied Franklin stove in the middle of the room.

Flames were crawling up the walls.

"Fire!" Jeremiah shouted.

He shook Rachel awake, and rousted other sleepers out of their blankets. Smoke poured into the basement. Jeremiah hustled the younger ones out into the cool April night. Some of the elderly he carried to safety. Others he shooed, pushed, or led from the flames attacking the tinder dry walls of the old church.

Rachel helped until she could no longer stand the smoke and heat.

Jeremiah swept her up, grabbed a blanket to cover her with, carried her outside, and placed her on the ground beyond the flames and smoke.

"You all right?" he said.

"I'm all right," she answered between choking coughs.

"I'll be back."

"I'll be here."

Jeremiah dashed away, and returned with his arms full of a young mother and her baby son. He placed them on the ground beside Rachel. She spread her blanket over them. The mother hugged her whimpering baby.

Jeremiah turned back toward the burning building. The front wall was caving in.

"Big Boy!" Rachel shouted.

Jeremiah jumped aside in time to avoid being buried under the tumbling wall of fire, and covered his face with an arm to ward off the heat of the roaring flames.

Rachel ran to him and wrapped her arms around his waist. They clung to each other as the charred walls sank into the church's basement.

Agonized cries and shouts of relief mingled with the terrifying crackle of the gluttonous flames devouring the little white church. Only minutes before, two dozen people were sleeping there. Three of them didn't survive. A little girl and her younger brother got separated from their mother and couldn't find their way out. Their hysterical mother struggled to go back into the flaming church for her children. She was restrained by friends who knew she couldn't reach them because of the devastating heat. The third person who died was an elderly man who suffocated in the stifling heat.

Jeremiah watched the last wall collapse into the basement. He gave his head a sorrowful shake. He didn't know how many people he carried to safety. He had done what he could, saddened by the loss of the church and those who died.

All around him, survivors wept, hugged, huddled together, consoling, or rejoicing that they escaped the flames, seeking comfort in each other's arms.

"I shoulda killed 'em," Jeremiah said to Rachel. "I shoulda killed the bastards!

# CHAPTER NINE

Morning splattered the still smoldering rubble with brilliant sunshine. Jeremiah stared at the heap of ashes in the hole in the ground that yesterday was the church's basement. Buried under the still smoldering ashes were the two small children and the old man whose bodies couldn't yet be recovered because of the intense heat. His eyes filled with tears because he couldn't save them.

"Are you the man they call Big Boy?"

A plump young white man was striding toward him with his hand out.

Jeremiah hesitated. He didn't mind when Rachel called him Big Boy, but he bristled when anyone else did.

Never before did a white man want to shake his hand.

"I guess I am," he said.

"I'm Orville Sims." Sims was a bespectacled

twenty-seven-year-old bachelor. He attended seminary and was ordained into the ministry in St. Louis. Fifteen months before, he was assigned to his first pastorate at the Wyandotte Methodist Church.

"I'm the preacher here," he said. "I want to thank you for what you did last night."

Jeremiah studied the haggard face of the young minister holding out his hand. He didn't feel right about shaking it, but he did.

"Some folks died," Jeremiah said.

"I was called away and didn't get back in time to help," Sims said, "What I hear, a lot more would have died if it hadn't been for you."

Jeremiah shifted uncomfortably from one foot to the other.

Sims said, "On behalf of this church, I want to thank you, and wish God's blessing on you."

"God's blessing?"

"Yes, sir."

Jeremiah thought about that. "Is that the same God my mama used to be prayin' to? And the one I heard LouEtta prayin' to the day I was hauled away, traded for a mule? And my wife, LouEtta–she was all time talkin' to God 'bout somethin'. Reckon could this be the same one?"

"We worship only one God."

"Uh-huh." Jeremiah glanced around, surveying the devastation of last night's fire. "You lost your church house."

"God willing, we'll rebuild the church, but the lives you saved could never have been replaced."

God again, Jeremiah mused. Where was God when the church house was burnin' down?

Sims turned away. "Thank you again," he said. "This church, and this whole town, owe you a debt of gratitude."

Jeremiah took a last look at the mound of rubble, the smoldering remains of what, a few hours before, was the little white church.

Etched on his memory was the face of the man with the knife-scarred cheek. "Maybe someday I see 'im again," Jeremiah said to himself, watching the departing back of the young preacher. "Maybe that God of his– Maybe someday."

Weary of waiting for strangers to work out what was going to happen to him, Jeremiah told himself it was time to move on. Time didn't belong to him. The more he wasted idling on the banks of the Kaw River, the longer it would take to find his family.

From the ash heap of the demolished church, he lifted his eyes to the west. How far you reckon it is to Nicodemus?

He turned away and saw Pastor Sims and Rachel clustered with half a dozen other people. He wondered what they were up to, but kept walking. More important matters were bulging the walls of his mind.

He heard Rachel call to him. He paused.

Sims stepped forward. "Mr. Higgins, they want somebody to come to a meeting."

"Who does?"

"A group of Wyandotte black people."

"You say black people?"

"Yes. Your friends here." Sims nodded toward the group. "They say you're the one who should go to the meeting."

All eyes focused on Jeremiah. They respected his imposing physical stature and quiet demeanor and looked to him for leadership.

He was still working on a response when someone said, "How about it, Big Boy?"

"They'll listen to you," another said.

Jeremiah was not sure.

Rachel tugged at his sleeve, and nodded as if to say, "You can do it, Big Boy."

The young minister moved away.

Jeremiah looked at Rachel as if not sure it was a good thing to do. She gave him an encouraging smile and a nod and watched him step away.

It didn't take long for Jeremiah to find out he wasn't invited to the meeting to share what intelligence he brought with him. The handful of black citizens, all men and former slaves, faced him from a half circle in the parlor of the Baptist Church parsonage. They showed no interest in what he had to say and didn't ask him to say it. Their intent was to pummel Jeremiah with their protests against his "bunch of lazy, ignorant no-goods" who invaded the tranquility of what they considered their territory. They wanted him to carry their threatening message to his fellow refugees camped on the banks of the Kaw River.

The Reverend Josiah Skates was in charge. Gray, heavy-set, and sixty-two, Skates made it clear the slaves weren't welcome in Wyandotte, Kansas. As a leader of the black community who had lived there for several years, he stressed that he and his friends were "disturbed by the turn of events that filled our city with slave trash", renouncing the refugees of whom he was once one.

"We don't need any trouble here," Skates said to the rhythm of the bobbing heads who shared his sentiments. "Everything was just fine until a flood of you ignorant blacks with no jobs and no money came pouring in here."

"You make us all look bad," said his fist-shaking neighbor.

"What we need," shouted a hysterical little man, "is for you to take your bunch of rabble-rousers and clear out of Wyandotte!"

"Go back to where you came from!" another put in.

"You ain't our load to carry!" another shouted.

Jeremiah was stunned by their belligerent attack against their own people. He got to his feet and planted a glare of disbelief on the faces of the group. He went away, having uttered not a word.

"Kansas," he said to himself as he trudged along. "The promise lan'. Maybe Nicodemus the only place in Kansas where black folks don't get treated like Mississippi slaves."

Sims and the others awaited his return from the meeting and greeted him with expectant faces.

Rachel got to him first. "What they say, Big Boy?"

Another said, "What they gonna do?"

Jeremiah took a deep breath. "They don't want us here. They want us to go back where we come from."

After a moment heavy with silence, a man shouted, "We don't need 'em!"

"We get by!" another chimed in.

Reverend Sims raised a calming hand. "Let us not be hasty in our–"

"We make our own way!" the man near him shouted.

Jeremiah counseled himself. "It's time to move on."

# CHAPTER TEN.

Jeremiah was glad he didn't tell Rachel he was leaving. She'd miss him sooner or later, he guessed. She might even worry about him when he didn't show up for breakfast. But she'd have tried to talk him out of it, and he didn't want to hear it. Or she might want to come with him. Either way, he could do without the bother.

He liked Rachel, and he liked having her around, but he didn't owe her anything. No explanation why, no nothing. Without her to worry about, he could travel faster, and he'd wasted too much time already.

Last night he couldn't sleep for thinking about it. That's when most of his thinking got done, when it was quiet. He could line things up and study them and see if they made sense.

What he decided made sense. Striking out on his own made sense. He was tired of waiting around for somebody to tell him what he could or couldn't do. He made up his own mind what he was going to do, and when to do it made sense. That was what kept him awake--thinking.

He slipped out of camp before daylight. He took with him a blanket and a bag of parched corn, and a few biscuits he tucked away from last night's supper the church women were good about bringing.

Everything west of Wyandotte was still brown and dry, not green and lush like Mississippi in April. Prairie dogs skittered around clumps of sagebrush. They eyed him closely, but kept their distance. He shivered a time or two at the sound of a rattler's chilling warning. Off in the distance he heard the yip-yip of a coyote scrounging for breakfast.

It was lonesome on the Kansas prairie, but Nicodemus was out there some place, and Jeremiah promised himself things would be better once he got there.

"The new Eden," they called it. His mama taught him about the old Eden, about Adam and Eve and that snake--about the apple they ate off the tree that God told them to keep their hands off of. They ate the apple anyhow, and God kicked them out of the Garden of Eden. He wondered what this new Eden would be like. Would there be wily snakes, and trees with apples God didn't want folks messing with? He'd find out when he got there. When he got there, he'd stop walking.

Toward noontime the sun bore down so hot that sweat popped out on his forehead. Jeremiah paused in the shade of an Osage orange shrub, and raked a sleeve across his face. The bag of biscuits and corn was tied to his waist with a cotton cord. His stomach was empty. He was tempted to eat a handful of corn, but decided not to just yet. He was reminded of times when he was hungrier, and he had to make it last now. Like in Vicksburg when he didn't eat for two days. He could hold out a while longer until he got some place for more. He didn't know when nor where that would be, but he didn't want to ask anybody for anything.

Half a dozen huge black birds floated overhead between himself and the cloudless blue sky, keeping an eye on him. Vultures. Jeremiah knew about vultures. Lolling around up there, eight-foot wings hardly moving like they weren't paying attention. Waiting for him to die. Waiting for him to collapse under the sweltering sun, so they could swoop down and rip his body to shreds with their razor sharp beaks and claws.

"Give it up," he said to the hovering predators. "You ain't gettin' me."

Up ahead he spotted a stand of cottonwoods and smelled the welcome scent of water. He knew about water too. Every time he tried to escape from Logantree's plantation he made for the creek running through the land. When the bulldozers came looking for him, he headed for the water. The bloodhounds couldn't pick up his scent on the water. One time he almost made it, but the bulldozers caught him and dragged him back and threw him in the box.

He was anxious to get to that water and soothe

his dry throat, and maybe rest a bit in the shade of the cottonwoods. Just long enough to catch his breath, then he'd be off again. Like when he clung to that barber pole back there in Vicksburg. He didn't know how far he walked, but he could feel his strength slipping away. If he stopped to rest it would only–

What was that? He jerked his head around, listening hard. Some kind of commotion behind him. He couldn't tell how far back, but the sounds were getting louder and closer. Dogs? Maybe a pack of coyotes. No, they weren't coyotes. He knew the sound. Bloodhounds! The blood-curdling howls had shot terror through his running-away body. On somebody's trail, he guessed. And horses. Hard-pounding hoof beats. More than one horse. Maybe a dozen men on horseback. Baying hounds frothing at the mouth. The sounds of trouble.

Jeremiah had no reason to run. The days of fear were behind him. He was a free man now, and nobody had any cause to hunt him down. Still, instincts of a lifetime of slave drivers' abuse took control, and told him to run.

Jeremiah ran. The faster he ran, the closer and louder grew the threatening sounds of hoof beats and baying bloodhounds. He knew they would overtake him in minutes. The saber-toothed dogs would be tearing at his heels. He stretched his long legs, fighting weariness, pulling up the dregs of energy that kept him on his feet. His lungs were near to bursting. He reached down deep, calling up all the strength in his big body to help him make it to the water ahead of the dogs. Once there, he'd dive in and stretch his lungs underwater for longer than he knew he could. He told himself the hounds would lose the scent, the men would ride on past, and he'd be safe.

He knew better. Lynch mobs were made of men with a thirst for blood, and they didn't care who it belonged to. The hounds might lose interest, unable to track the scent, but the men wouldn't be satisfied until their thirst for blood was quenched.

"Lord o' mercy!" Jeremiah said, recalling a plea of his mother's. "Get me to the water!"

Rachel was worried. She hadn't seen Jeremiah since he returned from that meeting last night. She wondered if something happened there that caused him to not show up for breakfast.

The camp was abuzz with reports of a white girl in town who was raped the night before. Sheriff Minnick and his deputies stormed into camp.

Rachel's worry got bigger.

"Ain't no secret blacks are born stealing," Minnick announced to the migrants huddled together around the campfires. "And God knows what else."

Every man in camp was a suspect. All of them shivered, along with their wives and children, at the threats of the vengeful sheriff.

"There's a guilty man some place among you," Minnick went on, "and you may as well tell us who he is."

Nobody identified the man, causing the incensed sheriff to order his men to "spread out and bring him in."

With guns and sniffing dogs the deputies ransacked the shacks and tents for the culprit who committed the heinous crime. Minnick would bet it was "a lead pipe cinch" the criminal was hiding somewhere in the camp.

The sheriff was a short, dried up man of fifty. Dressed in black from head to toe, a round hat, boot tops nudged his knees. His handlebar mustache twitched when he talked. "We know he's here," he said in a hoarse whiskey voice.

It was eleven years since the end of the Civil War set the slaves free. Still, when the white man spoke with an angry voice, the black man cringed. Now, they were drawn together by the sheriff's threat, trading whispered questions, casting fearful glances at the deputies turning the camp upside down.

One of the deputies leered at Rachel with a menacing gesture. She defiantly stood her ground. He raised a hand to strike her, then shoved her aside. He kicked over a pot of soup simmering on an open fire as he stalked away.

"If anybody knows who the guilty man is, you better speak up now," Minnick threatened. "We ain't leaving here till we find him."

Not a head turned and no eye blinked. It was like all breath was used up and the wind forgot to blow.

"All right," said the scrawny sheriff. He pushed his hat down on his head until it hid the tops of his eyes. "All you men line up over here in front of Deputy Hannibal," he said. "Hannibal is the one with the bull whip."

Hannibal was a burly man with a bloodshot right

eye. He cracked his whip a time or two with a fiendish laugh, striking fear in the hearts of the campers. Many times before they'd heard the crack of whips, felt the pain of their sting. They braced themselves for what they feared now.

"Hannibal's gonna to use that whip on every man here," Minnick said, "three lashes across the backside, until somebody confesses, or till we find the bastard that raped that poor little white girl."

A deputy touched the sheriff's arm and whispered something to him.

Minnick spat a streak of tobacco juice while he thought about what the man told him. His piercing black eyes scanned the crowd, looking for someone who was supposed to be there. He hadn't found him.

"Where's the big one?" he said.

Rachel froze. She was standing a few steps left of the sheriff. She knew who he meant by "the big one". Jeremiah wasn't there, so that made him the prime suspect. She knew he had nothing to do with it. She just knew. But in the mind of the sheriff, not being there made Jeremiah guilty.

Minnick's question was greeted with total silence. "I said where is the big one?" he shouted in a rage and shoved a black man to the ground.

The man, flat on his back, raised his arms to protect himself. "I don't know, sir," he said in a trembling voice.

"Well, somebody knows," Minnick bellowed, "and they damn well better start talking right now!"

From somewhere in the crowd came the thin voice of a man who said he'd seen the big man take off on foot heading west.

"When was that?" the sheriff demanded.

"Early, 'fore daylight. Prob'ly too far gone by now."

The sheriff turned away and his deputies followed. "We'll catch him," he muttered. To the crowd, he said, "You better hope we catch him. If we don't, we'll be back. Somebody's gonna pay for this!"

Rachel watched the sheriff and his men mount up and ride away in a cloud of dust. She didn't know where Jeremiah was, but she knew he didn't rape that little white girl. She also knew the sheriff didn't care whether Jeremiah was guilty. He was going to make somebody "pay for this".

Jeremiah's breath came in labored gasps, but he dared not stop to rest. His body ached, but his only chance of escaping the dogs was to get to the water before they did. He pulled the last morsel of strength from his body and kept running. They had no reason to come after him, except that he was black.

Kansas City, Wyandotte, and Topeka were brimful of former slaves. More were arriving every week and those towns could no longer accommodate them. Even some frustrated abolitionists, unable to solve the problem of "what to do with them Nigras", falsely charged them with crimes, threatened them with flogging or prison, hoping fear of arrest or punishment would force them back to where they came from. Black was bad.

Jeremiah ran until he stumbled into the water.

It was not a river, as he thought, but a small pond only a few feet deep. He plunged into it at full stride.

He hardly hit the water before the hounds bared their teeth and leaped in after him with blood-curdling snarls. Jeremiah fought them as hard as he could until three men with clubs and a rope sloshed into the water and laid hold of him.

"Get that rope on him!" the sheriff ordered from the bank.

Jeremiah struggled to keep his arms free, but his exhausted body could no longer fight. The deputies tied his hands, drew a noose around his neck, and dragged him up out of the water and onto the bank. They shoved him toward a cottonwood tree, tossed the loose end of the rope over a limb, and stretched his arms above his head.

"Lay it on him, Hannibal!" the sheriff shouted.

Two men stripped Jeremiah to the waist, and Hannibal began lashing his bare back with the rawhide whip.

Jeremiah felt the blood oozing down, soaking the tops of his pants. He gritted his teeth so hard to keep from crying out he thought they might crumble. He had done the same when Logantree's overseer Gorbus whipped him for running away.

"Run, boy!" Gorbus taunted, ripping Jeremiah's skin with the lash. "Let's see you run now, boy!"

Never did he give Gorbus the satisfaction of hearing him utter a sound.

Hannibal didn't hear him cry out either.

"No need to kill him, Hannibal," a hawk-nosed man named Linus said.

"He needs a good killin'," Hannibal sneered between lashes.

"We ain't plum sure he's the one that done it," Linus said.

Jeremiah's body went limp from the beating and Hannibal wrapped the whip around his left arm.

"Well, he may not be the one, but he's the one that run. Anyhow," Hannibal said with an evil laugh, "he'd prob'ly done it if he had the chance."

"All right, boys," the sheriff said. "We done what we come to do. Let's get back to town."

"You gonna leave him hanging there?" Linus said.

"Linus, you always was soft on them niggers," Hannibal said, mounting up. "You want him down, you cut him down."

Linus, a skinny man with black-rimmed glasses, moved his horse over and cut Jeremiah's hands loose. Jeremiah slumped to the ground, barely conscious. As they rode away, he heard Hannibal threaten, "You may be free, nigger, but you rape another little white girl, you gonna be dead."

Jeremiah struggled to a sitting position with his back against the tree. He worked his hands free and rubbed his wrists where the rope left ugly red welts. He lifted the noose from his neck, crawled to the pond, and rolled into the water, and floated with his face barely above the surface. Its coolness relieved some of the pain, and washed the blood from his lacerated back. A two-foot green snake wriggled toward him. With no time to move out of its path, he dared not even breathe. The snake crawled across the bridge of his nose. Jeremiah didn't blink till the snake slithered away.

He took a deep breath, climbed out of the water, and collapsed on the bank. His body relaxed and he slept. For how long he didn't know. Waking slowly, sore and stiff, he shook his head clear. At his side he heard body-wracking sobs, and felt the softness of trembling hands caressing his wounds.

Fearing for what might happen to Jeremiah if they found him, Rachel's instincts had compelled her to follow when the sheriff and his men rode away. She ran as far and as fast as she could for as long as she could, but she was soon unable to keep the riders in sight. She kept going, following the sound of the hoof beats. When she could no longer hear them, she followed what she hoped were their hoof prints. With no thought of how far she had run, she was determined to keep going until she reached Jeremiah, no matter how long it would take to get there. With no idea where that might be, she knew if the sheriff found him first, Jeremiah would need her.

She heard the pounding hoof beats of the horses on their way back to town, and ducked behind a wild rose bush until they passed. Again she started walking, running when she felt strong enough.

She knelt beside Jeremiah and gently touched his battered body.

"Rachel?" Jeremiah asked, his voice a breathless whisper.

"Why would God let them do this to you, Big Boy?"

"What you doin' here?"

She removed her head scarf, soaked it with water

from the pond, and swabbed his wounds. "Stay still," she said. "I know you never done nothin'. Why he let them do this to you?"

"Ain't no God in Kansas. No God no place for folks like us."

"Yes, He is! God is for ever'body."

"No. Only God they is, is white folks' God."

"No, Big Boy. He all we got."

"Ain't no promise lan' either." He spoke slowly, thinking out what he wanted to say. "Only promise lan' was the one Moses looked at from the mountain top. He spend all that time bringin' the people out of slave country, then God don't let him in. Whose God you s'pose he is?"

"God is God. He ever'body's God."

"My mama told me God look after black boys same as white. I reckon He too busy to look after this one."

Rachel sniffled and wiped her eyes. "What you gonna do, Big Boy?"

"I don't know yet." He stretched an arm to see if it was still working. "I don't know. But I don't think I be lookin' for God, 'cause He ain't lookin' for me."

"I look after you, Big Boy."

He took a moment to study her tear-stained face. "You good at that." He touched her face with the tips of his fingers. "You good at takin' care of folks."

She grinned through the tears. "Somebody got to take care of you till you big 'nough to take care of yoself."

He nodded. "How you get here?"

"Runnin' hard. That many horses leave lots of tracks."

Jeremiah fell silent. For a long time Rachel watched him think.

"I can't stay here no more," he said. He got to his feet, brushed himself off, and pointed his eyes west. "Nicodemus out there some place, and I got to go find it."

"I go with you, Big Boy."

"No. You stay here."

"No! I go with you!"

"You don't know 'bout me."

"I don't care. I go with you."

"You go on back yonder, back where the white folks are. They the boss. They the smart ones. They know what's good for us. You go on back now and listen to what they tell you."

He turned away with at a determined pace.

Rachel ran after him and threw her arms around him. She pleaded with him to let her go with him.

Jeremiah caught her by the shoulders and held her at arm's length. "You go 'way from me. I ain't nothin' but a no-good nigger, not stoppin' people from burnin' the church house down, rapin' little white girls. Not good enough for God to–"

"No!" she cried. "You didn't rape that little girl!"

"They say I did."

"I know you didn't, and you know you didn't. You too good for that."

"I ain't good."

"Yes, you are! You couldn't stop them fools from burnin' the church house down. Somebody paid 'em to do it. They's minds was made up and there was nothin' you could do about it."

Jeremiah shook his head, searching for words, trying to make her understand she'd be better off away from him.

"It don't matter none," he said.

Even so, hearing the sound of defeat in his voice, he knew it did matter. He hoped one day he'd come face-to-face with the scar-faced man who set fire to the church. That mattered. And what about Hannibal? He could feel his muscles growing taut, insides churning with anger, the heat of vengeance surging through his body. That mattered too.

He wanted to strike back at what his mama taught him was evil. People whippin' people. Killin' people. Not lettin' 'em do what they got a right to do. Out there in the middle of what was the heat-and-dust cursed nothingness of Kansas, what could he do?

He flung Rachel aside. She fell to the ground. "You go on back now," he said. With long strides he struck out toward the west.

"Don't leave me, Big Boy." Like a prayer on a gentle breeze her voice came to him. He could feel the tears that burned his eyes. He tried to find something to help him understand what was happening.

Rachel's pleading wasn't for herself only, but for him too. She committed herself to him. Strange feelings raced through his big body. Feelings he hadn't known since long ago he was denied the joy of LouEtta's warm closeness.

It wasn't the first time he had thought about it. He felt an urge to hold Rachel the way he used to hold LouEtta, but LouEtta got in the way. LouEtta was always there when the pain struck, giving him strength to fight off the demons.

"Don't leave me, Big Boy."

In thirteen years no one had spoken to him that way. Not since the day they hauled him away in that wagon with his hands tied behind him, his legs shackled, when he watched LouEtta run behind the wagon until she collapsed in the dust. "Don't leave me, Jeremiah!" she cried.

LouEtta couldn't see the tears he shed then. He hid them now from Rachel. How could he leave her there--crying and alone--with night time coming on? His mama would turn over in her grave if she knew he left her there on that Kansas prairie all by herself. No telling what might happen to her.

"Don't leave me, Big Boy!" The words rang in his ears. Slowly he moved to where she knelt on the ground. He dropped to his knees beside her. Gently he drew her to him. Like a man who for thirteen years hadn't known the comfort of a woman's arms.

She did not resist. He wrapped her in his blanket and she slept. All night he sat by the fire. Watching over Rachel. Thinking.

# CHAPTER ELEVEN

*"I'm goin' back."*

The sun was hardly up, but Jeremiah hadn't slept. Hannibal beat him because he was black. That wasn't reason enough for his body to be ripped with a bone-tipped lash.

Rachel knuckled the sleep from her eyes. "Back where?"

"Back where we come from. I gotta go back."

"Why you goin' back?"

"That Hannibal--he beat me with a whip. I gotta go back."

"They kill you, Big Boy."

"They tried that a'ready."

"I come with you."

"No, you stay here."

"Big Boy!"

"No. Gonna be some trouble. Nothin' you can

do."

"You gonna be there, I gonna be there."

He gave his head an impatient shake. Telling her to stay put was a waste of breath. Her mind was made up. She was going with him. He struck out on the way back to Wyandotte. Rachel scrambled to her feet and followed.

On the plantation there were times when Jeremiah could have killed Gorbus for his cruel lashings with his bull whip. Had he killed the malicious overseer, they'd have hanged him. What would have become of LouEtta and the boys?

After those hooligans set fire to the church, he was mad enough to kill all four of them. He spared them.

For a lifetime he fought with himself before he finally lost the battle, and yielded to the urge to seek revenge against Logantree for killing his mother.

He didn't know when nor how, but he knew the time would come when he and Hannibal would meet face-to-face. The blood of another human being had never stained the hands of Jeremiah Higgins. Now, though, his anger reached the point where the need to get even was driving him to settle the score with the whip-wielding bully.

"No tellin' how many other folks he whipped 'cause they black," Jeremiah counseled himself. "By night time, maybe they be throwin' dirt in my face, but I gotta do somethin'." Even the chance of being buried in a shallow grave, or maybe thrown to the dogs, could not blunt his determination to pay back the man whose whip left scars on his back.

News of Jeremiah's thrashing stirred the camp as a warning of what would happen to anyone who got out of line. "Let that be a lesson to you," Sheriff Minnick threatened on his return to the camp. "You break the law in this town, you pay the price!"

Still some distance from the camp, Jeremiah and Rachel heard voices in mournful song. Always there were the voices, thanking the Lord for what He gave them, or pleading for release from oppression. As they drew near the camp, they smelled the tantalizing aroma of vegetable stew simmering over open fires.

"Here come Big Boy," they heard a man say. The news had spread like an echo. The big one was back.

"What you gonna do, Big Boy?" someone wanted to know.

Jeremiah didn't answer. He kept a steady pace toward the town, past the hovels and campfires, beyond the anxious faces of those hovering around them. All eyes were trained on the big man who returned with a job to do, and was dead set on getting it done.

"You gon' get 'im, Big Boy?"

Three men fell in beside him, trying to match his long strides. A dozen more followed, and within minutes, no man was left in the camp.

Rachel knelt beside seventy-eight-year-old Maudie Webster. Maudie clutched her three-year-old great-grandson to her breast, protecting him from what to her smelled like trouble.

"Lord, have mercy!" Maudie cried, and didn't bother to wipe her eyes. "What gon' become of us?"

Jeremiah spoke not a word. The men followed and didn't ask where he was going or what he was going to do when he got there. Whatever the big man was about to do, they figured it needed doing.

At the edge of town a log building squatted with a rough-hewn board nailed to a post in front. Scrawled on the board in black paint were the words "Sheriff's office."

From inside the building, Hannibal Crutcher peered out the front window. His eyes got big, He had trouble believing what he was looking at.

"They're comin', sheriff!" Hannibal screeched.

Cyrus Minnick, sitting with his straight-back chair leaning against the wall on its two back legs, concentrated on the latest edition of the Wyandotte Herald.

"Who's coming?" he said without interest.

"Them blacks!"

Minnick tossed the paper aside, bounced the chair off the floor, and joined Hannibal at the window. He saw a big black man leading a mob of angry former slaves.

"Well," he sneered, "it looks like one whippin' wasn't enough for that one."

Hannibal grabbed his whip from a peg on the wall and snapped it at the sheriff's feet. "I'll fix that black bastard!" he said. "He'll wish them buzzards had et him alive when I get through with him."

"Get the other boys," Minnick said. "Tell them to bring their guns."

Hannibal took off out the back way with the whip wound around his left shoulder.

Minnick stepped out the front door in a show of

what he thought would show intimidating authority against a rabble of ignorant Negroes. They wouldn't dare challenge the law of Wyandotte County.

He was wrong.

As the freedmen drew closer, the sheriff pulled aside the front of his coat and revealed the pistol holstered on his right hip. In his left hand he held a shotgun.

Jeremiah never broke stride. Behind him were one-hundred-twenty-nine axe, shovel, and tree limb wielding freedmen. Some carried torches of dried tree limbs they lit along the way. They waved them above their heads as they closed in on the sheriff's office.

Twenty paces from where the sheriff stood, Jeremiah raised a hand and the procession halted.

Minnick pointed the shotgun at Jeremiah. "Hold it right there, black man!"

"We come to get Hannibal," Jeremiah said.

"He ain't here," said the sheriff, relieved that they hadn't come for him. "Go on, get out of here," he shouted, waving the shotgun, "or I'll blow you to hell!"

A voice from the crowd said, "He can't kill us all."

"He done it too, Big Boy," another said, "same as Hannibal."

"Throw a rope on 'im!" said a third man.

The sheriff froze as the mob closed in. He glanced about, looking for his men with the guns. They weren't there.

"That damn Hannibal!" he swore to himself. "I should've gone after 'em myself."

No sooner did Hannibal clear the back door of the sheriff's office than he was overcome by a strange curiosity to witness what was taking place out front. He peeked around a corner of the building, shot through with fear at sight of a mob of irate freedmen. Sweat broke out on his brow, and his hands began to shake.

"We come to get Hannibal," Hannibal heard the big man say. He recognized Jeremiah as the man he horse whipped, the man he wouldn't dare face without the support of the sheriff's posse behind him.

And those fire-breathing blacks. They wanted his blood! His whip would be no defense against them. He couldn't fight them all, even if he wanted to, and he didn't want to. It was different whipping one man with his hands tied above his head to a tree, a man who couldn't fight back.

Hannibal could feel his stomach begin to tumble with the fear of having his arms ripped from their sockets by an angry mob. He slunk away, leaving the sheriff alone to deal with the vengeful blacks.

"I'm warning you!" Minnick shouted in a panic. Jeremiah kept coming. "One more step and I'll—"

"Burn it down!" somebody yelled, and another man tossed a flaming limb onto the roof of the log building.

Running for his life, the sheriff scrambled back inside. He threw the crossbar on the door, grabbed a second shotgun from the rack and began filling his pockets with shells. His plan was to barricade himself in the jail and make a stand. Kill the big man first, he thought, and the others would turn tail and run. But the flames were already burning a hole in the tinder dry roof, and smoke was pouring into the building.

Minnick's frantic thought was to save himself. He tossed the guns aside, burst out the back door, and took off at a dead run.

"There he goes!" someone shouted.

Jeremiah watched the hungry flames lapping at the walls. "Let 'im go," he said.

"Let 'im go?" was the confused response.

Burning the sheriff's office was little consolation since Hannibal was the man Jeremiah came for. Getting to Nicodemus was more important than chasing after the sheriff.

Sunrise found Jeremiah hiking west. He told Rachel the night before he was leaving Wyandotte.

She said, "Me too."

He expected no less of her. He gave his head a solemn nod and took off at a brisk pace. She fell in step beside him. Nicodemus was a long way off, Jeremiah conceded, and, though his plan was to travel alone, he couldn't deny Rachel's good company.

Nursing his anger toward Hannibal, he could still feel the pain of the roughneck's lash. Hanging the despicable Minnick, as Jeremiah's fellow refugees were eager to do, would lay no pain on the back of the cowardly man with the whip.

"Someday I meet up with him again," he promised himself.

His journey with Rachel took them past the cottonwood tree where Jeremiah suffered the lashes of Hannibal's whip. Seeing it again stoked his eagerness to settle with the vicious Crutcher. But that would have to wait.

Rachel couldn't look at the tree. She knew how Jeremiah was hurt there. She wanted to erase from her mind the tragic scene where she found him, bleeding from Hannibal's ruthless beating.

Jeremiah didn't have to look. The event was indelibly etched on his mind, and he wouldn't forget it.

Somewhere west of Leavenworth they met up with a group of twenty-two people on their way to Nicodemus. The group was escorted to Baxter Springs by an ex-slave named Benjamin "Pap" Singleton. Singleton planned to establish an all-black settlement in southeast Kansas.

The pilgrims, disappointed in what they found there, were faced with the prospect of returning to the South and the drudgery they had escaped. They didn't want to go back to the life they hated before. Still, some reasoned, if they returned to the plantations they would have a roof over their heads and food a plenty. The alternative was to continue their trek to the uncertainty of northwest Kansas.

"We come this far," was their final decision. "Ain't no turnin' back now."

Jeremiah and Rachel were invited to join the group on their journey west. Two days later the company trudged into a town they heard somebody call Lawrence, Kansas.

Jeremiah never heard of Lawrence. He was told it had something to do with the legend of John

Brown. Nor did he know the state of Kansas hadn't always been referred to as "the promised land". Border clashes between pro-slavery and anti-slavery activists from 1854 to 1865 earned the state the infamous label of "Bleeding Kansas". With devastating frequency, Missouri's slave-holding sympathizers attacked the rabid Kansas abolitionists, adding fuel to the struggle of whether Kansas should be admitted to the Union as a slave state or a "free state".

The most vicious band of guerrillas was commanded by a twenty-year-old renegade named William Clarke Quantrill. A native of Ohio, Quantrill's allegiance was to neither North nor South, though he sympathized with the Confederacy in its defense of slavery. In the dead of night, Quantrill led his marauders across the line from Missouri in ravaging assaults on Kansas towns along the border. They robbed, looted, and killed without cause.

Lawrence was the Free Stater's territorial headquarters, a prime target of Quantrill's forays. On April 21, 1863, he swept into Lawrence with four hundred of his guerrillas in a savage pre-dawn attack. The carnage lasted for hours, and when it was over, dozens of homes had been looted and burned, business places were pillaged, bank vaults emptied, and one-hundred-eighty-three men lay dead.

Despite the devastation, the spirit of the Lawrence citizens never flagged. They rebuilt their town, defying the fury of public officials who scorned the blacks as inferior to whites. Many local citizens assumed the responsibility of providing for the freedmen's welfare, and Lawrence became a major gathering place for refugees on their way west. Without the help of the caring people of Lawrence, many would have perished.

Quantrill continued his rampage of killing and looting until 1865 when he was gunned down in a raid on a Kentucky town. Violent and destructive as his life was, Quantrill was hailed as a hero by pro-slavery sympathizers.

In 1867 the Kansas Pacific Railroad established a water station at Ellis where its tracks ended. Travel from Ellis to Nicodemus, thirty-five miles north was, therefore, on foot, by horse drawn wagon, or horseback.

Jeremiah had neither horse nor wagon, and he didn't know how far it was from Lawrence to Nicodemus. But, from blacksmithing during his time in Lawrence, he earned enough for train fare from Lawrence to Ellis, and he couldn't wait to get there. The caustic blare of the train whistle signaled time to climb aboard. Jeremiah and Rachel eagerly did so.

When the train screeched to a stop at Ellis, Jeremiah was surprised to see groups of former slaves already camped along the tracks. They had pitched small tents and built shoddy lean-tos for shelter. Many of them fell victim to an epidemic of measles, unable to continue their trek west.

As did the people of Lawrence, the citizens of Ellis brought food to the refugees to tide them over till they could move on.

Rachel escaped the illness. She stayed busy caring for those who were stricken, serving them vegetable soup and fried bread, and whatever she could do to make them comfortable.

One of the few men unaffected by the epidemic, Jeremiah scavenged for wood to keep the camp fires burning. It was by one of those fires that Rachel found him, down on one knee as though in prayer. He poked at the coals with a sycamore branch, stirred the embers, and added a stick of wood now and then.

"You look like you wore out, Big Boy," she said.

The sound of her voice brought a smile to his face. "To a frazzle."

"You better be gettin' some rest 'fore you keel over dead."

"I gonna live a while yet."

On Logantree's plantation there was little time for rest. Sometimes Jeremiah felt like he'd never been anything but tired. Working the fields from sunrise till dark, Jeremiah often collapsed on his straw pallet without supper. LouEtta knew he was hurting. She massaged his back and shoulders to work out the pain.

To Rachel, he said, "I don't see you doin' any restin'."

"I'm all right."

"You a good woman, Rachel."

With the trace of a smile, she said, "I know."

Jeremiah jerked his head around, listening hard for something he heard behind him.

"What?" Rachel said.

"I hear somebody say Hannibal."

"Hannibal?"

"The one that put the whip on me."

"If he–"

Jeremiah put his hand out and she helped him listen.

Hannibal Crutcher was a barrel-chested, gap-toothed forty-year-old with scraggly black eyebrows that came together in a point above his camel hump nose. His pock-marked, unshaven complexion was further marred by a bloodshot right eye and the absence of a left ear. The ear was ripped off by a rebellious black man before Hannibal beat him to death.

Crutcher rarely smiled but laughed often, a vicious, deprecating laugh that shot bolts of fear through the former slaves, conditioned by generations of quaking at the sound of the white man's voice.

Hannibal was a former slave driver, deputized by Sheriff Minnick to "negotiate" with the freed slaves. After the refugees' march against the sheriff's office, Hannibal waged a campaign of vengeance that resulted in his beating to death four black men.

Even the sheriff responded to local citizens' complaints of Hannibal's excessive brutality. They demanded his "disciplinary measures" be less severe. The hot-headed whip wielder protested. Minnick ordered him to make himself scarce in Wyandotte County. In a blind rage, Crutcher attacked the sheriff with his whip. The attack left Minnick prostrate and seriously injured.

Hannibal took off on horseback. Somewhere east of Ellis, Crutcher fell in with a group of former slaves from Tennessee. He cracked his whip and demanded more food and drink for himself when there was hardly enough to go around. Exercising what he considered his white superiority, he assumed control of his fellow travelers. He also imposed himself upon some of the younger women, and intimidated one and all with the threat of the rawhide bull whip snaked around his shoulder.

"No, Hannibal!" Jeremiah heard a woman cry. "Leave me alone!"

"Like hell I'll leave you alone, you black bitch."

The sound of the menacing voice rang in the ears of Jeremiah since the day he was tied to that tree.

"You may be free, nigger," Crutcher sneered as he rode away that day, "but you rape another little white girl and you gonna be dead!"

Anger became vengeful rage flooding Jeremiah's body. Bearing yet the scars of Hannibal's lashing, he bounced to his feet.

"Where you goin', Big Boy?" Rachel said.

"You wait here."

He started walking in the direction of the commotion till he saw people huddled around camp fires, cringing from the threats of the bully with the whip.

And there he was. The brutish Hannibal was holding the whip in his left hand. With his right hand he pulled at a young black woman who was screaming at him to "get away from me!"

Sullen faced onlookers were afraid for the woman who fought to free herself from the clutches of the whip-wielding monster. They dared not interfere lest he use the whip on them.

Ten feet away stood Jeremiah. "You Hannibal?"

Startled by the interruption, Hannibal spun around. He saw the towering black man staring into his bloodshot eye. "Who the hell wants to know?" he sneered.

The woman took advantage of the distraction, twisted her arm free, and hurried away.

"I hear somebody say Hannibal," Jeremiah said, "I need to know if that you."

"I'm Hannibal," he smirked. "What's that to you?"

Jeremiah knew the answer, but he asked any way. "You the one that does the whippin' for that sheriff back there?"

Hannibal's sneer disappeared. He squinted for a closer look at the face of the man staring him down. He had no trouble recognizing Jeremiah as the black giant he whipped with his hands tied to that tree. The one who led the mob against the sheriff's office the night Hannibal ran for his life.

From the bowels of evil escaped a vicious laugh. Hannibal snapped the whip a time or two, reminding the crowd who he was.

"You're that black bastard that raped that little white girl, ain't you?" he said.

"I never raped nobody."

Hannibal lashed out with his whip and struck Jeremiah across the back.

"I should've finished the job before," he snarled. He swung again and wrapped the lash around Jeremiah's legs. Jeremiah went down. The bone-tipped leather ripped Jeremiah's shirt as he rolled away.

Again the bully lashed out. Jeremiah grabbed the whip and yanked it from his grasp. He bounced to his feet, and struck Hannibal a solid blow to the head with the butt of the whip. Hannibal plopped to the ground, squirming in pain.

Jeremiah laid the leather on the cowering thug.

Hannibal pulled his knees up to his chin, whimpering like a wounded pup. Naked without his whip, blood spurted from Hannibal's lacerated body. Screams of pain burst from the twisted lips of the cringing roughneck.

When Hannibal no longer moved, Jeremiah flung the whip into a wild rose thicket. He turned away without a word and left the bully sprawled out with his face in the dust. He neither knew, nor cared, whether Hannibal was dead or alive.

The circle of onlookers were relieved that the brutal slave driver was beaten with his own whip. They watched with wordless nods of gratitude as Jeremiah walked away.

Rachel fell in beside him. She placed a hand in his as they walked.

Jeremiah's score with Hannibal was settled. How long would it be before he did the same with the scar-faced one?

# CHAPTER TWELVE

In 1848 Jessup Campbell loaded up his family and moved by wagon and horseback from Illinois to Kansas. He staked out twelve thousand acres of ranch land. In the winter, eight years later, Jessup lost his battle with pneumonia. He left the ranch to his son Ethan.

Ethan was the eldest of Jessup's five sons. Two of his brothers died in the Indian wars. The other two were killed at Shiloh, fighting on the side of the Confederacy.

Ethan loved the land. Over the years since his father died, he bred, fed, and drove thousands of cattle to the railhead at Ellis from where they were shipped to markets in the east.

Two of Ethan's cowhands, Pete Milsap and Finis Birdwell, were rounding up strays on the eastern slope, urging them back to the grazing herd.

Birdwell's gaze fell upon something he thought

didn't belong there. He draped his lumpy body forward in the saddle and scanned the low-lying hills for strays. Again he squinted into the distance and couldn't believe what he saw. Yep. It sure as hell looked like it belonged some place besides Kansas. Against the dry sod, he saw what looked like a thin shadow drawn with a pencil on the sunburnt prairie.

"Hey, Pete!" he said.

Milsap, slender and berry brown, turned to look at what his partner was so excited about. Maybe it was a cow dropping a calf.

"You see that?" Birdwell said.

Pete followed Finis's pointing finger to what Finis wanted him to see.

"I see it," Pete said

"What the hell is it?"

"Freed slaves from the South," Milsap said. "Mr. Campbell said more of them would be coming. I guess that's them. Likely headed for Nicodemus."

"What's Nicodemus?"

"It's that town over by the river some of them started a while back." Pete wheeled his mare about and spurred her toward the ranch house. "Let's go. Mr. Campbell needs to know about this."

Campbell grew up on the land his father fought and bled for. Before the Treaties, Jessup battled Sioux, Cheyenne and Comanche. Through it all, Jessup held on to the twelve thousand acres he claimed. He overcame the hardships which might have defeated a lesser man. Even so, fight as he did, Jessup couldn't defeat the ravages of pneumonia to which he succumbed at the age of seventy-eight.

Ethan planted his father's body next to his mother in the family burial plot on the hillside north of the house.

Lean and leathery as the saddle he sat on, Ethan took another look at the line of immigrants snaking across the prairie. He believed slavery was wrong. No man should be bound against his will. He fought against it during the war.

In the battle of Wilson's Creek, he lost half a shoulder to a cannonball fighting with the Free Staters. His father fought to defend every inch of his land. He wouldn't have tolerated such an invasion of strangers. Jessup defended his land against hostile Indians, pestilence, drought and disease to hold onto what was his. He sacrificed much to keep it, and never would he have relinquished to anyone what he and his sons had bled and died for.

"I knew they'd be coming," Ethan said of the newcomers, flanked by Milsap and Birdwell. "But I never had any idea there'd be this many. What do you make of it, Pete?"

"Danged if I know, Mr. Campbell," Milsap said. "But if they keep on coming, planting crops, building fences– I don't know."

"It'll take some time for that to happen," Campbell said. "We'll give them free rein for a while. If they decide to settle on our land–"

"Yes, sir. What if they do?"

"We'll see. From what I hear all they want is a place where they can live without somebody telling them what to do." Again he said, "We'll see."

"Yes, sir."

# CHAPTER THIRTEEN

W. R. Hill's search for a place to establish his colony of former slaves ended at the point where Spring Creek flowed into the Solomon River. Except for its nearness to water, the location had few redeeming features. By the time Jeremiah arrived it had improved little.

What he found was an assortment of dugouts and sod houses, sprinkled about as if dropped from the sky, and settled where they fell. Beyond the settlement, black people, who learned their skills on the plantations, bent their backs hoeing, weeding, and planting. The government said they could call it their own if they lived on it and worked it for five years.

Not everybody who came stayed. Some of the less venturesome, after traveling many miles from nothing, expecting to find something they could cling to, returned "home" to the South. They resumed their former jobs on the plantations, rather than "live in holes in the ground like rabbits". The more hardy souls, while emitting sighs of disillusionment, determined to "tough it out", distressed as they were by the arid nothingness of the open prairie.

"We make do," they vowed. They battled drought, blizzards, and swarms of crop-chewing grasshoppers. They clung to their dream of independence. Trusting in their God, they told themselves that one day they'd reap the rewards of their labor.

In the words of Leila Amos Pendleton, a chronicler of the time: "...may He who holds Creation in the hollow of His hand, and yet marks the sparrow's fall, behold, and see the Negro, persecuted and afflicted, cast down and almost destroyed, still clinging to the faith once delivered to the saints, still looking up, through blood and tears, to the Eternal God."


The first settler in Nicodemus was a former slave named Simon P. Roundtree. A Baptist preacher, Roundtree distributed the first circular to "the colored people of the United States". He urged them to come start a new life in the "great Solomon River valley of western Kansas". Roundtree, like Singleton, traveled the Southland, encouraging former slaves to migrate to the West, and "throw off the yoke of degradation and oppression."

In 1877 Roundtree established the first church in Nicodemus. He was there to welcome the sturdy travelers who trudged the dreary miles from Ellis to reach the promised land and encouraged them not to give up. "Keep working," he admonished. "I know it ain't easy, but nothing good comes out of nothing. Think back to where you come from, and be glad you ain't there no more!"

The parched earth between Ellis and Nicodemus promised little that stirred in the heart of a weary traveler any joy for having come. Except for an occasional stand of cottonwoods, Osage orange, or box elder trees along the banks of struggling streams, a sweltering Jeremiah harbored faint hope that things would be better farther west.

Indeed, sight of what he heard described as "the new Eden" gave Jeremiah cause to wonder whether it was a fruitless, heart-sinking journey. Was the new Eden nothing more than a spurious plot born of greed to lure innocent former slaves to a place where they anticipated plenty, but found only desolation?

No tree bearing forbidden fruit did Jeremiah see in the new Eden, but snakes there were aplenty. Some snakes nested in the thatched roofs of the dugouts carved out of the prairie. It was not uncommon for the settlers to shrink from a wriggling snake dropping into their living quarters through the ceiling.

Jeremiah anticipated "schools, churches, and places of business." What he found was powder dry soil, trampled underfoot for untold ages by the sharp, pounding hooves of stampeding buffalo. Soil that offered little hope of becoming fertile enough to grow corn, beans and potatoes.

With hard bound determination, the hardy

freedmen stuck it out. "We ain't goin' back! We gonna stay here and dig this groun'!"

All they had to dig with were shovels, hoes and pick axes they were able to carry with them. Laboring for endless, backbreaking hours from daylight till dark, praying for rain that didn't fall from cloudless skies. They worked the thirsty dirt, preparing it for seeds, nurtured with water carried in wooden buckets from the Solomon River. Sight of a green sprout peeking through the cracks of the stubborn sod was cause for celebration.

Jeremiah was surprised to find people "living in holes like rabbits", as some derided them. The "holes" were called dugouts, pick-and-shoveled into the sides of small hills, or into dirt that dared them to dig.

Most common was a rectangular space about fifteen feet long, fourteen feet wide, and six feet from floor to ceiling. Because of the earth's sloping contour, much of the dugout was above ground, enclosed by blocks of dried sod. Forming the roof was a center pole running the length of the dugout with tree branches and brush to cover it. On one side of the dugout, they carved steps in the sod that led down to the bare dirt floor of the one room. The fireplace stretched across one wall of the dark, windowless room. Oddly, it was cool in summer and warm in winter.

Over time, some dugouts were replaced by more easily constructed sod houses with walls made of strips of prairie sod two feet wide and four inches thick.

A network of tangled grass roots held the strips

of sod together to prevent their crumbling. A few pioneers rounded up enough lumber to build wooden doors and window frames. Some even found glass for the windows.

It was into one of the sod houses that Rachel was invited by Margaret Morgan, whose family arrived in the early days of Nicodemus settlement.

"It don't amount to much," Margaret said to Rachel, "but it belong to us."

Margaret was a heavyset woman of fifty-three with a beehive of gray hair piled on top of her head. On the plantation she had labored in the cotton fields beside her husband, Silas, and still found time to bear seven children. Four of her sons were taken from her by the master when they grew to be six years old, and were put to work in the cotton fields. When the war was over, her two older sons ran away with the jubilant shouts of "I'm free!" She hadn't heard from them since.

The only child Margaret had left was a daughter named Seddy. Seddy was a few years younger than Rachel's twenty-four. Rachel was assigned a corner of the room where she and Seddy shared a pallet near the fireplace.

Seddy had a baby son who was born on the way to Nicodemus. Rachel didn't know whether Seddy had a husband, but she never saw one, nor did she hear anyone mention his name.

Seddy spent time sewing things for her toddler son, but she wasn't a very good seamstress. Rachel learned the skill from her mother, and offered to help with Seddy's sewing. The young mother accepted the offer, and Rachel soon became known in the village as "the sewing lady". Other people began bringing her items to mend or sew. Compensation was minimal, since money in Nicodemus was a scarce commodity. Even so, Rachel kept busy, and whatever she received for her efforts paid for her keep.

One night after Silas and Seddy fell asleep, Rachel and Margaret sat quietly by the crackling fireplace. Rachel was mending a coat she promised to have done the next day. Margaret studied the images in the dancing flames.

"You and Mr. Higgins," Margaret said. "You know each other a long time?"

Rachel was startled by the question, since never before had Margaret spoken Jeremiah's name to her.

Since they arrived in Nicodemus, she and Jeremiah had seen little of each other, except for Sunday church services and Wednesday night prayer meeting. She kept busy with her sewing, doing what she could to help with cooking and cleaning around the house.

"Mister Higgins," whose imposing physical stature and tranquil disposition drew to himself respect and authority. By no wish of his own, Jeremiah became a leader in the community.

Even Simon Bridges recognized Jeremiah's quiet influence among the settlers. Bridges solicited his aid keeping the peace, settling disputes, and generally "being around when something needed doing." That and his blacksmithing chores left Jeremiah little time for socializing.

"No, ma'am," Rachel said to Margaret with a modest smile. "We don't know each other a long time."

"Uh-huh," Margaret grunted with a suspicious nod. "I notice the way yo eyes light up, and the secret little smile that sneak across yo face when he show up at meetin', or when somebody mention his name–like now."

Rachel lowered her head and covered her face with a hand to hide the embarrassed smile she knew was there. "We met on the boat from Vicksburg," she said.

"Uh-huh," Margaret grunted. She was satisfied that something was taking place between Rachel and Mister Higgins she wasn't supposed to know about. She was eager to find out what it was.

"Do he know?" Margaret said.

"Know what, ma'am?"

"Do he know when you lookin' at him with them sad cow eyes you tellin' the whole wide worl' you crazy in love with that ol' boy?"

Rachel laid her sewing aside, unable to concentrate on the coat she was mending. "I think he know, but–"

"But what, chile?"

"He told me to go 'way from him."

The older woman emitted another meditative grunt. "You might oughta be thinkin' 'bout doin' that."

"Why you say that?"

Margaret took a moment to think about the words she'd use.

"Man like him," she said, "don't matter where he is or what he doin', you see it in he's eyes plain as day. He's mind is always like someplace else, lookin' fo' somethin' or somebody. Like he ain't gonna rest till he find it."

Rachel gave her head a solemn nod. She'd seen that look, puzzled that Margaret had noticed. "I–don't know what it means."

"That's what I seen in it. It mean you stay 'way from him, or one day he gon' break yo' sweet lil' heart."

"Yes, ma'am."

"Do what I tell you now, or you gon be sorry you don't."

"Thank you, ma'am."


At no time during his travels was the mind of Jeremiah free of the image of his wife LouEtta. Wherever he came up on a group of refugees, his eyes instinctively searched the dark faces for one that looked like her. None of them did. Once, in Topeka, when the train stopped to take on water, his heart leaped with hope at the sight of the back of a woman's head he thought was LouEtta's. He was disappointed when he discovered the woman was not LouEtta.

The first day he saw Nicodemus, Jeremiah looked out over the barren land, the dugouts that some who preceded him called home, and the bent backs of workers in the fields. With fading hope, he said, "So this is the promise land."

He gave his head a bewildered shake, breathed a curse upon Simon Bridges for lying to him about what he'd find there. He searched for something that would make him glad he came. He didn't find it. "Well," he mused with resignation, "it's Kansas.

And this is Nicodemus." Surely, he tried to convince himself, somewhere among all the black folks who kept coming, he'd find LouEtta and his boys.

The first person who grabbed his hand in a hearty shake was a sixty-two-year-old refugee from Tennessee named Silas Morgan. Thin, slightly stooped, and cordial, Silas said, "I'm mighty proud to see you. It ain't milk and honey here, but we makin' do."

Jeremiah asked Silas about his wife and sons. "Two little boys," Jeremiah said, recalling them as they were when last he saw them.

Silas shook his woolly gray head. "No, sir," he said. "I don't b'lieve I know anybody with that name."

Jeremiah's inquiries brought only negative responses. People, especially the women, sometimes exchanged furtive glances and shook their heads. Delilah Withrow, the woman who served him hog fat and yams at the Emanuel Baptist Church in Vicksburg, showed no sign of recognition when Jeremiah asked her about his family. Nor had he, in need at the time of something to feed his growling stomach, any recollection of Delilah. Avoiding his eyes, she uttered only, "Huh-uh" before turning away.

When Silas came in from the field for supper, Margaret asked him, "What that big man lookin' for?"

"Some woman," Silas said. "I don't 'member her name."

"You think the girl know?"

"Know what?"

"'Bout the woman he lookin' fo'.''

"I dunno," said Silas, "but I ain't tellin' her." With a sharp look at his wife, he said, "And you don' need be doin' no gossipin'.''

"Maybe I won't tell her," Margaret counseled herself when Silas turned away. "An' maybe I will."

"Higgins!"

Jeremiah looked up from stoking the forge and faced a scrubby cowhand on horseback. He recognized him as Henson, a Bridges wrangler.

"Mr. Bridges said for you to come up there," Henson said.

His skill as a blacksmith kept Jeremiah busy beating metal into hoes, shovels, picks and plow shares. He was called on to assist in the construction of business buildings, the church, and houses, and was depended on as one who "knows how to do."

One day he confessed to Rachel that he didn't always know "how to do," but learned by doing what had to be done.

"You good at it," Rachel said.

"You get good at it," Jeremiah said with a grin, "when ain't nobody else doin' it."

At their encounter in Vicksburg, Bridges had recognized Jeremiah's potential as a peace keeper among the former slaves. "Look me up if you get that far," Bridges said.

Jeremiah didn't. Instead, it was Bridges who sought Jeremiah's help in settling a land boundary dispute between two farmers. The matter was resolved peaceably, enhancing respect in the community for Jeremiah.

"Mr. Bridges?" Jeremiah said to Henson.

"Yeah. Says he needs to talk to you."

Henson rode away, shaking his head. He wondered what a white man like Bridges would have to say to a slave.

Jeremiah wiped his hands on a rag from a hip pocket, and took off up the hill to the big house. Half way up, he paused for a look back to where he came from. "Long way up for a talk," he told himself, resuming the climb. "Same way goin' down I reckon."

The two-story stone house Hill awarded Bridges for helping settle the newcomers at Nicodemus. Bridges was administrator of the settlement, and the house stood as a symbol of his authority.

Jeremiah found Bridges waiting in the parlor. The room was furnished with heavy oak chairs and tables. Against one wall was mounted a gun rack with half a dozen rifles and hand guns next to a huge stone fireplace. Facing the fireplace were two cane-backed rocking chairs. Bridges was seated in one of them, chewing on an unlit cigar. He waved Jeremiah into the other chair.

"You can be a big help to me," Bridges said without saying hello. With a curious eye he studied the big man staring back at him.

Bridges had not forgotten their first meeting in Vicksburg when he learned that the woman now hidden away in a back room of the big house was Jeremiah's wife LouEtta. Bridges grew certain over time that, had Jeremiah known of her whereabouts, he'd have stormed up there and torn the place apart to rescue his wife. Bridges knew he was treading on thin ice by inviting Jeremiah into his home, and made sure LouEtta stayed out of sight. She didn't know Jeremiah was there.

Despite the risk of being discovered, Bridges needed help controlling the growing numbers of freedmen migrating to Kansas. He knew Jeremiah was the man for the job.

"I can use a good man to keep watch over the black folks," Bridges said, waving the cigar like a wand. "Somebody to keep an eye on them so they don't cause a lot of trouble."

He paused, trying to determine with a studied look into the eyes of Jeremiah Higgins, whether the black man suspected Bridges was harboring his wife. He half expected Jeremiah to attack him on the spot, as a guilty man senses that everybody knows of his guilt.

Bridges decided boldness was the best approach. "You're the man I need for that job, Higgins."

Jeremiah gave his head a dubious shake. "I never told nobody what to do," he said.

On the plantations Jeremiah had been bossed and ordered to do this and do that by bullying overseers, one of whom Bridges once was. He had no taste for treating other people as he was treated.

"There likely wouldn't be much call for that," Bridges said. "After the way you handled that dispute with those farmers, the people have a lot of respect for you. Knowing you're the one they'd be answering to, they'd think again before they stepped out of line." He struck a sulfur match to his cigar, inhaled the smoke like it might be the last time he'd ever do it, and blew out a gray fog. With a steady gaze, he said, "You saved my neck back there when Dinsmore and his mob tried to hang me. I won't forget that, and I know you're the man for this job." Bridges puffed and blew. "This is wild country, Higgins. Full of outlaws, renegade Indians, cattle rustlers, and bank busters. A man could get himself killed just for looking sideways at a stranger. People need to be protected from lawlessness. I need you to take care of that for me if it happens. You're the only man I know who could do that."

"Take care of–"

"I could round up some hired guns," Bridges went, waving his cigar with an off handed gesture, "but I'm sure your people would rather have one of their own looking out for them. Higgins, I want you to carry the law in Nicodemus."

Jeremiah wondered whether it was a request or a demand. Either way, he wasn't comfortable and showed it. Bridges plunged ahead. "Can you handle a gun?"

"No, sir. I don't know 'bout guns." He'd seen enough of guns when the slave patrols rounded him up and dragged him back to the box for trying to run away.

"Well," Bridges said, "the time might come when you'll need to know. You might think about leaning, just in case."

"Mr. Bridges, I–"

"There's a man who rides by here once in a while on his way to someplace else. He's spent the night at my place a time or two. His name is Earp, a famous lawman in these parts. If he's a mind to, he could teach you what you need to know to do the job around here."

Bridges stood up, letting Jeremiah know the conversation was over, and that he had just been assigned a new responsibility--keeping the peace in Nicodemus.

"Earp won't spend much time in one place for long any more. But next time he comes around, I'll put him onto you."

# CHAPTER FOURTEEN

The dusty street of Nicodemus was lined with houses of sod, some of logs, a few of stone. There too was Simon P. Roundtree's Baptist Church. In the early days, Roundtree conducted services on the banks of the Solomon River, "close to the water" for baptizing converts.

Next to the church stood Fisher's General Store, providing the ladies with bolts of gingham, and needles and thread for Rachel's mending. Also available at Fisher's were sacks of flour that, once empty, became aprons, dish cloths, and head scarves for the women. Fisher's supplied men's straw hats, shoes, and overalls.

Nicodemus was a frequent stop for cattle drovers who urged their herds to the railhead at Ellis, where a longhorn steer brought forty dollars, compared to ten in Texas. And so a viable market for the settlers' crops was open to them. What the settlers ate, they raised from the soil. If there were beans, corn, or other products left over, they were sold to merchants in Ellis. The merchants supplied them to cattle buyers from the east who flooded the town, drummers, and wranglers who pushed their herds up the Chisholm Trail from Texas. Nicodemians began to reap the rewards of their labor, enjoying the better things in life which they had long been denied.

Jeremiah was well aware of the incident to which Bridges called "saving my neck". After the first few weeks, disappointed and angry at the promoters who misled them about the wonders of Nicodemus, a group of the settlers decided they were "not gonna take it anymore." Worked into a frenzy by Roscoe Dinsmore, a burly, balding man of forty-nine, half a hundred of his irate sympathizers followed his lead in an attempt to exact retribution for their suffering. Simon Bridges, the target of their venom, was the semblance of power from whom the mob sought revenge.

Roscoe grabbed a rope, waved his huge arms in a windmill motion, urging his cohorts to follow him up the hill to the Big House. They were hell-bent on dangling Simon Bridges on the short end of a neck-scrubbing rope.

Jeremiah wasn't among them. He knew Roscoe as a hot-head who talked big and loud, who carried through with none of his previous threats. With that in mind, Jeremiah suspected nothing serious would come of Dinsmore's protest this time either.

Bridges wasn't so sure. He paced uneasily back and forth in front of the window overlooking his front yard. He saw a mob of angry, fist-shaking blacks threatening to break his door down. He saw Caleb Hooley twirling a rope with a noose at one end. Bridges grabbed his throat as if already feeling the noose tightening around his neck.

Even so, Bridges was less frightened than angry. How dare these simple former slaves rise up against the man who helped them escape the oppression of the southern plantations! What right had they to hang him from a tree in his own yard over whose limb he now saw Caleb toss the loose end of the rope?

The former slave driver still struggled with the fact that he could no longer crack the whip over these people. He couldn't order them about as he did in the fields, like the slaves they once were. He also couldn't believe they mustered enough courage to attack their benefactor.

He wrestled with the notion that they were now free men who had grown beyond cringing at the sound of the white man's voice, taking matters into their own hands-- "getting even" for the wrongs they suffered.

Bridges cringed at the thought of facing the angry mob. Yet, ingrained in his brain was the conviction that he was superior to the black man. He convinced himself that he need only venture forth and protest loudly, bark a few sharp orders to this gathering of unruly, child-like Negroes, and they would slink away. Like scolded pups with their tails between their legs, they would, wish they hadn't come.

He was wrong.

Bridges gathered what was left of his courage, flung open the door, and stepped onto the porch. He raised his right hand, and demanded quiet and attention. He got neither. Within seconds he was surrounded by half a dozen incensed black men who laid hold of him, tied his hands behind his back, and dragged him away to the cottonwood tree from whose limb the noose already swung in the breeze. They looped the noose over the head of the struggling Bridges and tied the other end of the rope to the halter of a mule.

Roscoe raised a hand, ready to slap the mule on the rump, causing it to leap forward, jerking the frantic Bridges off the ground with a snapped neck.

That was the plan. But there was an unexpected stir among the crowd. All eyes were drawn to the leisurely approach up the hill of Jeremiah Higgins. Jeremiah heard the commotion from down below and decided this time he'd misjudged the grit of Roscoe Dinsmore. The crowd gave way as Jeremiah strode to where Simon Bridges shivered with the noose around his neck, his face contorted with fear.

"Get me out of this, Higgins!" Bridges shouted. "These people are crazy!"

Here was a white man, Jeremiah counseled himself, sweating with a noose around his neck, trembling with fright, pleading with a former slave to rescue him from the brink of death. Here too was a handful of black men dead set on ending the life of the unscrupulous ex-slave driver for the lies he told them about what life would be like in Nicodemus.

Jeremiah could muster no sympathy for the

frantic Bridges. The curtain of the past was shredded. Across his memory raced the agonizing parade of hunger, the lashings, the shackles, the misery of his long legs cramped into a box, and the never-ending pain of losing his family--and the sentence of having tearfully watched while his mother was raped and beaten to death by the beastly plantation owner. It all came rushing back like a river out of banks. In the back of his mind dwelt the cry for vengeance, to fight back, to take from the white man the comfort and privilege, and the peace of mind taken from him.

Jeremiah knew what his peers were going through. He lived with an urge to kill, to obliterate evil. He couldn't care less whether Simon Bridges lived or died. Bridges was the enemy, the dispenser of tyranny and punishment, and his fellow freedmen believed he deserved to die.

Jeremiah's sympathy was with the men who held the rope. But he knew lynching Bridges would serve no purpose beyond the momentary pleasure of watching him die, ridding the world of the devil's footman.

To Dinsmore, Jeremiah said, "What's this about?"

"He lie to us!" a man said.

"He lie!" the mob echoed. "Ain't no seeds, no hoss, no plow. He tol' us they was churches and school houses."

"Ain't none of them!" angry voices shouted.

They'd had enough of Bridges's deception. They rolled their hatred into a concentrated effort to exact retribution.

"Why you doin' this now?" Jeremiah said.

A slender young woman stepped forward. "This mornin' Juliana's baby die," she said. She pointed an accusing finger at Bridges. "He tol' Juliana he get med'cine for to save her chile. He never got the med'cine. Her baby die."

Jeremiah gave his head a sorrowful shake. "Ain't no bringin' that little baby back." With a gesture toward the whimpering Bridges, he said, "Hangin' him won't do it."

"You aimin' on stoppin' us?" Roscoe said.

"No, I can't stop you. If yo mind's made up, can't nobody stop you, but hangin' him won't fix nothin'. You still got no seeds, no hosses, and no plows. Still be livin' in holes in the ground, and wouldn't be no washin' his blood off yo hands."

Again he studied their faces. Eyes, uneasy now, lowered to their shuffling feet. They didn't want to be part of a lynch mob, but Dinsmore convinced them it was the right thing to do.

"You want to go back to slavin'?" Jeremiah said. Their response was a shame-faced shake of heads. "This ain't the promise lan'," he said. "They ain't no new Eden either, but this chunk of dirt is all we got. We come all the way from nothin' to nothin', but this nothin' is better'n the nothin' we left back there. What we got now belong to us. If we go to work and make somethin' out of it, ain't nobody can take it away from us."

With a motion of his head he let Bridges know he wasn't forgotten.

"He ain't been straight with us," Jeremiah said, "but hangin' him won't make it no better. We still gotta do what we gotta do for our own selves." And with that he walked away, headed back down the hill.

The crowd fell silent, but Roscoe was not ready to give up. "We gonna let him talk us out of it?" he shouted. "C'mon! This man lie to us. We need to do what we come to do." His eyes traveled around the gathering, seeking support. Those who, moments before, were loud in their vengeance, now turned away. Roscoe was left standing alone.

"Give it up, Dinsmore," Bridges sneered. "You got no guts for this without a crowd."

Roscoe flashed him a defiant look, eying the mule, fighting the urge to slap it on the rump and see Bridges swing with that noose around his neck.

"You a lucky man," Roscoe said. "You a mighty lucky man you ain't gaspin' with a limp neck. You was one breath away from it." He jerked the noose from around the sweating Bridges's neck, and loosened the knot around his wrists.

"I had my way," Dinsmore spat, "you be danglin' with yo feet off'n the ground and yo eyes buggin' out."

Bridges rubbed the red marks the noose left on his neck. He knew how lucky he was to be alive, but a scathing glare was all he could conjure up for Dinsmore.

With unsteady strides, Bridges moved away toward the Big House.

On his way down the hill, Jeremiah met Rachel on her way up.

"What they doin' up there, Big Boy?"

"Hangin' Simon Bridges."

"You gonna let 'em do it?"

He never broke stride. "I done all I can do."

"You know he need hangin'." She fell in step behind him, trying to keep up.

"He need hangin'," Jeremiah said. "But the devil don't need no help doin' it."

Rachel shaded her eyes from the sun's glare for another look back up the hill. "Big Boy," she said, pointing. "Look."

Jeremiah stopped. He saw the crowd turning away. "Look like even the devil know when to quit."

"Big Boy."

He paused half way down the hill. Somehow he knew she'd call to him, wishing she wouldn't, hoping she would.

"I love you, Big Boy."

"Don't say that to me."

He'd tried to put her beyond his thinking. Her smiling face kept popping up in the glowing embers of the forge. And sometimes in the night, thoughts of Rachel disturbed his sleep.

"I do love you, Big Boy."

Trying not to think about Rachel was like asking the sun not to shine. Jeremiah never abandoned hope, though he knew the chances of finding his family were fading. Still, every time a new group of refugees arrived in Nicodemus, he searched their faces with the hope of finding those he'd recognize. In spite of that, in the space he reserved for LouEtta, more and more often he now saw Rachel.

He fought the urge to run to her, take her in his

arms, and share the warmth and comfort of holding her close. He dared not, as though his feet were rooted to the ground. On his mind lay a burden of guilt, for his dedication to the memory of his family was as strong as ever. He couldn't be the man Rachel said she loved.

"Go 'way from me!" he said, and took off down the hill.

"Big Boy!" she cried to his departing back.

In spite of Silas's warning not to "gossip", Margaret's curiosity outlived her patience, and she couldn't wait to again broach with Rachel the subject of Jeremiah Higgins. Slicing hog fat into a pot of boiling collard greens, from the corner of an eye she watched Rachel at work with needle and thread.

"You see Mr. Higgins?" Margaret said casually, as if only making conversation.

Rachel, stitching a patch onto a pair of pants, payed her little mind.

"Mr. Higgins?" Rachel said. "Did I see him when?"

"Lately."

Rachel shook her head. "He stay busy."

"Uh-huh." Margaret sliced the pork and stirred it into the pot. "He a married man?"

"He tol' me he married once."

"Humph," the older woman grunted. "Man like him, he married once, he married all time." The itch to tell Rachel more of what she heard from Delilah kept nagging at Margaret, sorely tempting her to scratch it. Finally, unable to resist, she said, "You know why he come here?"

"Same as ev'body else, I guess–for somethin' better."

"That a part of it."

"Part of it?" Rachel started paying attention.

"Why he come. Other part is, he come lookin' fo' a woman."

Rachel pinned her with a sharp look.

"Be careful, chile," Margaret said. She placed a sympathetic hand on the arm of her young friend. "Don't go lettin' yosef in fo' a worl' o' hurt."

"I know about his wife and sons," Rachel said.

Margaret was privy to another newsy tidbit she felt compelled to share with Rachel. "I gon tell you somethin' you don't know," she said in a low, confidential voice. "Somethin' you go'n' not repeat to a livin' soul, y' hear?"

Wide-eyed with wonder, Rachel put her mending aside, and nodded.

"Delilah Withrow," Margaret said, "she say the woman he come lookin' fo' livin' in the big house up yonder on the hill. An' Delilah, she say ain't no tellin' what go on up there." She gave Rachel's hand a gentle pat. "I jus' thought you'd oughta know, chile."

"Yes, ma'am," Rachel's eyes studied her hands. "Thank you, ma'am."

# CHAPTER FIFTEEN

*"Watch his eyes!"*

October blessed the Kansas prairie with the relief of cool air. Anyone up and around before sunup that morning would have seen the rider in a black hat ambling his bay gelding down the middle of the Nicodemus Main Street.

He dodged a wave of tumbleweeds, and gigged his bay toward the blacksmith shop at the end of the street. A scruffy handlebar mustache hid his upper lip. Except for the white shirt, he was garbed in black. With the string tie knotted at his throat, folks could have taken him for a preacher or a school teacher. His enemies--those who still had breath in their bodies, remembered him as the legendary fast-shooting lawman of the West. His name was Wyatt Earp.

Earp's pursuit of outlaws took him far and wide, including occasional stopovers for supplies at

Nicodemus, where he struck up a casual acquaintance with Simon Bridges.

It was hardly past daylight when Earp pulled up at the blacksmith shop. To the big black man stoking the forge, he said, "My horse threw a shoe."

"We fix that," Jeremiah said.

"How much?"

"You got the old shoe, one dollah. No old shoe, two dollah."

Earp nodded agreement.

"You got the old shoe?" Jeremiah asked.

"No."

"Two dollah."

Earp glanced about, surveying his surroundings. Satisfied that all was well, he said, "How about you fix my horse, and I'll show you how to shoot?"

Jeremiah cast him a quizzical look.

"You Higgins?" Earp said.

"Yes, sir."

"Bridges says you want to learn how to shoot a gun."

"No, sir."

"You don't want to learn?"

"No, sir."

"Well," Earp said, turning away, "if you don't want to learn, I sure as hell can't teach you."

"Are you Mr. Earp?"

"Not many people call me that, but I'm Wyatt Earp."

"Mr. Bridges, he think I need to know how."

"He says you carry the law in this town."

"You think I need to know about guns?"

"Looks like a quiet town to me," Earp said, "but

you never know. There may come a time when a man needs the edge he can get with a gun."

Jeremiah gave his head a thoughtful nod. "All right."

"Watch his eyes," Earp said, and Jeremiah listened. With Earp's six shooter in both hands, Jeremiah pointed it at a fence post. He didn't like guns, and wanted nothing to do with them, but Bridges thought he needed to know. The lawman said he'd show him how. Jeremiah decided to give it a try.

"When you're facing a man," Earp said, "you'll have the advantage with your back to the sun so you can see his eyes. Watch his eyes. They'll tell you what he's going to do. Don't make any threats. He may talk his head off, trying to throw you off guard, but don't talk to him. His first move toward his gun is your signal and you've got to be ready. He may be faster than you, but with a good shot, you'll kill him."

Jeremiah pulled the trigger, the gun jerked in his grasp. The shot missed.

"Squeeze the trigger," Earp said. "If you jerk it, you'll miss, and he'll kill you. Aim for the chest. That's the biggest target."

After what seemed hours of repetitive practice, Jeremiah was losing patience.

Earp kept at him. "You're doing fine. Keep at it. You're getting there."

By the time Earp rode out of town two days later, Jeremiah gained confidence. But he was not convinced that what he needed to keep the peace in

Nicodemus was the Colt .44 Earp left without.

Jeremiah knew he wasn't cut out to be a gunman. He didn't even want to be. He placed the gun on a cottonwood stump and went back to pounding red hot metal into a plow share.

He would learn the truth of Earp's prediction: "There are times when a man needs the edge a gun will give him."

By the summer of 1879, many residents of Nicodemus upgraded their living quarters from dugouts to sod houses. Some houses were built with stone. A few had glass pane windows. No matter how sound their construction, however, always present was the threat of scorpions, insects, and snakes wriggling through the thatched roofs or porous walls.

One July day Jeremiah was busy repairing a weather worn hole in the wall when he became aware of a stranger riding his way on a mule in full harness. With little interest, Jeremiah regarded him as just another passerby on his way to someplace else. Then the mule stopped and snorted ten feet from where Jeremiah stood. There was no doubt in the mind of Jeremiah that he had seen the man before. It took less than a minute for him to recognize the stranger as the scar-faced one. He was the one who led the attack on him in St. Louis, and one of the four who set fire to the little church in Wyandotte.

A husky black man with sweat rolling down his cheeks slid off the mule and took a step to where Jeremiah was eying him.

"Man say you'd he'p me 'ith my broke down tater cart," the stranger said. "It quit on me a piece back. Lost a wheel."

Jeremiah studied the man's face. He was the one all right. Jeremiah promised himself he wouldn't get bit by the same snake twice. "I take a look at the wheel," he said.

"Good!" the man said with a broad smile. "At's good!"

"But the way I see it," Jeremiah said, "you ain't gon' be needin' no tater cart for a while."

"What yo mean?"

"You know what I mean."

With a steady gaze into the face of Jeremiah Higgins, the man said, "Why, you ol' Big Boy!" He flashed a big smile, hoping it would soften the threat he heard in the Jeremiah's words

"Uh-huh," Jeremiah said. "And you one o' them slimy bastards that burn the church house down."

"Why, I– That a long time ago."

"Not long 'nuff to bring back them two little chilluns and that ol' man what die in the fire."

The man made a move to run, but Jeremiah's words stopped him.

"No use bein' in a hurry. No place much to hide 'round here."

Jeremiah fought the urge to throttle the mule-riding stranger. "You got one choice," he said. "Back up on that hill behind you is the buryin' groun'. You can go there, or you can spend some time in my lockup till the judge decide to come 'round an' take you off'n my hands. The judge, he don't show up but ev' whipstitch, whenev' the notion strike. He ain't been here now since way las' fall. Buryin' groun' is the quickest way out. It's up to you."

Scarface was nervous. He shifted uneasily from one foot to the other.

Jeremiah watched him squirm.

"Now, come on, Big Boy," the man pleaded, his mouth twisted in a frenzied grin. "I got a wife and kids."

"Uh-huh. Lockup ain't too bad. Ev' day or two, if somebody think 'bout it, they slide a couple o' biscuits and a cup o' water under the door."

"I ain't the one, Big Boy," the man said. Beads of sweat popped out on his forehead. "Them other ones–they the ones that done it."

"Where they now?"

"Dead. They all dead. Shot down in a hold up."

Jeremiah was not impressed. "Look like you go'n' have to pay for all o' them too." He nodded his head, indicating it was time to quit talking and start moving.

"What 'bout my wife and kids?" Scarface whined.

"We'll send 'em word."

"An' 'at mule o' mine. He don't know nobody but me."

"He'll get acquainted."

Had Jeremiah responded to his inclination, he'd have bashed the man's head in, hauled him up to the burying ground, and called it good. He guided him, instead, to the tool shed next to the blacksmith shop that served as a "lock up". It had never been used for that.

On the way, Scarface spotted Wyatt Earp's .44 pistol on the cottonwood stump.

It didn't go unnoticed by Jeremiah. He jabbed him in the ribs, shoved him inside the shed, and threw the crossbar that locked the door from the outside.

"You gon' leave me in here, Big Boy?" the prisoner wailed.

Jeremiah strode away without a word.

Three weeks passed before the judge happened by. He deputized two men to escort Jeremiah's prisoner, tied on his mule, to the Graham County seat.

Word got back to Jeremiah that he was hanged for setting the church fire that killed the two children and the old man. With news of the hanging, Jeremiah learned the name of his prisoner. William Beckett. Beckett had no wife nor children, and the mule he rode into Nicodemus he stole from a farmer the day before.

Beckett's body remained unclaimed.

## Chapter Sixteen

"Mr. Higgins," Silas Morgan said, striding toward Jeremiah with an anxious look on his face. "Mr. Higgins," Silas said again, "I think you need to be goin' up to the big house."

"What's that, Silas?"

"They's some kind o' commotion goin' on up there."

"What kind o' commotion?"

"I don't know, but I seen a man ridin' that way that look like he gon' skin somebody alive."

Jeremiah tossed the hammer aside. "Who was the man?"

"He look like that Mr. Campbell you tell us 'bout."

"I'll go see." Jeremiah wriggled into his blue cotton shirt. For some reason, instinct told him to grab Earp's gun off the stump. He stuck it in his waistband and took off up the hill.

Simon Bridges was flat out on the floor of the Big House front room. Blood streamed from his mouth. Ethan Campbell was glaring at him with his gun drawn, ready to finish him off.

Bridges stared wild-eyed at Campbell, afraid the rancher might pull the trigger and splatter his brains all over his walls.

Jeremiah had done some work for Campbell and knew him to be an honorable man. He wondered what Bridges did to cause the rancher to take such drastic action.

Campbell offered a nod of recognition when Jeremiah showed up.

"Mr. Campbell," Jeremiah said, "what's the trouble here?"

Before Campbell could answer, Bridges blurted out, "He says I stole his cattle!"

"Did you? Jeremiah said.

"Hell no, I never stole his damn cattle!'

To Campbell, Jeremiah said, "Did anybody see this?"

"One of my hands," Campbell said. "He caught two Bridges riders cutting steers out of my herd and switching the brands."

"He's lying!" Bridges screamed.

"Where's your man, Mr. Campbell?" Jeremiah said.

"Outside."

"Let's call him in and talk to him." Nodding toward the pistol Campbell aimed at the sweating Bridges, Jeremiah said, "You can put that away. He ain't goin' no place."

Campbell shot a glare at Bridges, then slipped the gun into its holster. The rancher moved to the door. He motioned to a slender young man with a week's growth of beard, and the man stepped into the room.

"This is Sloan," Campbell said. "He's the one who saw them."

To Sloan, Jeremiah said, "Who did you see?"

Sloan hesitated, looked to Campbell for approval. Campbell nodded it was all right to talk to the black man.

"I ain't used to dealin' with niggers," Sloan said.

Jeremiah took a deep, patient breath and said again, "Who did you see?"

"It's all right," Campbell said to Sloan. "Tell him who you saw."

"I seen 'em outside," Sloan said.

"Do you know who they are?" Jeremiah asked.

"No, but I can show 'em to you."

Jeremiah motioned to Sloan to lead the way out the door and followed him. Sloan pointed out two rough looking cowhands lounging at one end of the wooden porch.

Jeremiah recognized them as riders for the Bridges outfit.

"Lock and Henson," Jeremiah said.

Sloan said to Campbell, "You need me anymore?"

Campbell said, "Higgins?"

Jeremiah shook his head and Sloan left.

Jeremiah and Campbell stepped back inside.

Recognizing an unguarded moment, Bridges got to his feet, made a move as if to rush Campbell, but backed off when the rancher went for his gun.

Jeremiah drew Earp's pistol from his waistband, and said, "Don't do it, Mr. Campbell."

"Kill him, Higgins!" Bridges screamed, writhing in fear of extinction. "Kill the lying bastard where he stands!"

Jeremiah knew Lock and Henson as trouble makers, suspecting they likely were guilty of Ethan Campbell's accusation. His respect for Campbell told him the rancher wouldn't go off half-cocked, and had a good reason for the charges against the quavering Bridges. Jeremiah had questioned the ethics of Simon Bridges in the past, but didn't confront him.

"Mr. Campbell," Jeremiah said, "You trust me to settle this?"

The rancher took a moment to reply. "His people stole my cattle. I aim to see that he pays for that."

"You'll get 'em back."

Campbell knew Higgins was a man of his word, but questioned whether he could deal satisfactorily with Bridges. "All right." He holstered his pistol. "But if this happens again–"

"It won't," Jeremiah assured him.

"–I'll handle it my way."

"You know, Mr. Campbell," Jeremiah said, eyes glued to those of the shrinking Bridges.

"I mind the time when I'd've gone to hell for this man. He helped me get to a place where I could be my own boss without worryin' 'bout bein' horse whipped, or locked in a cage."

As he talked, a thin, derisive smile of relief sneaked across the face of Simon Bridges.

To Bridges, Jeremiah said, "I've bashed a few heads for you when I had to, and twisted some arms."

Bridges chuckled, sure now that he was off the hook.

"But I ain't your slave, and you don't pay me enough to do your killing." Jeremiah slid Wyatt Earp's .44 across the floor. It came to rest at the feet of the cowering Bridges. "If you want him dead, you kill him."

Bridges froze. His eyes flashed at sight of the gun. He flexed his fingers, wishing he had the grit to go for it. But he was no good with guns and never was. Like Hannibal, the only weapon Bridges used on the plantation was a rawhide bullwhip.

Campbell stood alert, feet apart, right hand hovering near the butt of the gun strapped to his right thigh. He dared Bridges to go for the gun.

The frantic Bridges ached to try, but knew he couldn't beat the cattleman in a gun fight.

"Mr. Bridges?" Jeremiah said.

From somewhere in the silence of the moment rose a small voice.

"Jeremiah."

Soft, as if it came from far away, soundless as the spider spins its web, the word reached the ears of Jeremiah Higgins. The voice he hadn't heard for thirteen years. The voice he'd recognize in a chorus of a thousand voices. Over and over from the shadowy corners of his senses it had come to him during endless days of tireless searching. It called to him in the darkness of sleepless nights. "Don't leave me, Jeremiah!"

Jeremiah's heart leaped to his throat. No need to look for the face that went with the voice. Every minute of every day his vision of that face gave him the strength to go on, to go hungry, to sleep in soggy corn fields at the end of fruitless days of walking in shoes with soles worn thin. Through years he longed to see that face and hear that voice. Yes, he confessed, though hope had begun to fade, never had he allowed himself to give up. He still clung to belief that someday, somewhere he'd find LouEtta and his boys.

"LouEtta!" he breathed.

# CHAPTER SEVENTEEN

One of the first former slaves to board the steamship at Vicksburg for the journey to St. Louis was Delilah Withrow. Delilah was a huge woman of forty-seven who grew up in the fields of a Mississippi plantation where her parents died. She lost her husband and three children to the fever, agonizing that it didn't take her in their place.

Delilah had no idea what she would find when she arrived at Nicodemus. If life there was half as attractive as described by the fliers and promoters, it would be heaven compared to the humiliation she suffered as a Mississippi slave.

After the War, many freed slaves refused to perform the same tasks demanded of them by their masters. Frustrated planters, unable to plant and harvest crops without Negro labor, appealed to state authorities who passed laws establishing denigrating Black Codes by which the day-to-day activities of the freedmen were controlled.

Delilah hated those laws. Most of all she hated the arrogance of the landowners who portrayed themselves as parental overseers of the freedmen, and still claimed their "right" to treat them as slaves.

An imposing figure, with arms like thighs and thighs like oak stumps, Delilah flashed her dark eyes when she was angry. Her vitriolic tongue was known for ripping to shreds anyone who did her ill.

Even so, when Jeremiah asked her if she knew of LouEtta's whereabouts, her eyes softened, and showed no sign of recognition of the man she gave food at the Emanuel Baptist Church in Vicksburg. All she had for him was a solemn nod as she turned away. Recalling her first encounter with LouEtta, maybe sometime she'd share it with Jeremiah, but this was not the time.

Jeremiah was one of thousands of former slaves who went in search of their families from whom they were long ago separated by the war. LouEtta Higgins was one of them. Told that she was free to go where she wanted, she asked herself what that meant. Free to do what? To go where? Was Jeremiah not free also? If so, why hadn't he come for her and the boys?

Her wanderings led her to Vicksburg. One day at sunset, she was near to collapsing on the steps of the Emanuel Baptist Church. As the shadows lengthened into evening, she drew her sons to her, each seeking warmth from the other. What was she to do? Money she earned as a housemaid along the way was gone. Where was there a place for a former slave woman with two young sons?

In the midst of her pondering she heard a door open. She turned to see who was behind her. Filling the doorway she saw a large black woman, startled to find three people huddled together on the steps of her church.

The woman was Delilah Withrow. It was her Wednesday evening obligation to plan and prepare the nightly meal in the church basement for the homeless and hungry. Tonight would be her last at the church. Tomorrow she'd board a steamboat bound for a place called Nicodemus.

"We're not ready for you yet," Delilah said.

"Not ready?" said LouEtta.

"The meal. It's not ready yet."

"Oh, I didn't– What– A meal–"

"Are you all right?" Delilah asked.

"All right? Yes. My sons–we come a long way–"

Over her shoulder Delilah called to someone LouEtta couldn't see. A moment later an elderly black man with white chin whiskers appeared from inside the church. He moved to assist LouEtta, but her son Jacob said, "We take care of her."

Jacob and his younger brother Joseph each took their mother by an arm and helped her inside.

Delilah motioned them to a chair with a soft cushion, and the boys guided LouEtta into it. Delilah told the man to bring LouEtta a glass of water, and he did.

"Are you all right now, mama?" Joseph said. He was worried because his mother was the one who wanted to keep going when the boys suggested they stop to rest. It was as if she feared time might run out before they completed their mission.

With a faint smile, she nodded to the man who brought the water. They finished the first meal they'd had in two days.

Delilah arranged for them to spend the night in the church. The following morning, she accompanied them to the staging area. There they saw a boat preparing to steam up the Mississippi to St. Louis, on the way to a place called Nicodemus.

"Nicodemus?" LouEtta said when Delilah told her where the refugees were bound.

Delilah explained that Nicodemus was a settlement of freed slaves. Lou Etta consulted her teenaged sons, whose opinions she often sought in their travels. Together they decided Nicodemus could be no worse than Mississippi. They were encouraged by the hope that in Nicodemus lay their chances of finding their father and husband.

The boys may have forgotten Jeremiah since they were quite small when he was traded away. LouEtta did not forget. But she couldn't have been prepared for what awaited them in the land that Delilah told them was the new Eden.

"LouEtta!"

Jeremiah fought the urge to sweep her up and carry her away. His heart told him to forget Campbell and Bridges. His heart urged him to settle other matters first.

"Mr. Campbell," he said, "you said you'd trust me to handle this. I need you to do that."

Bridges weaved unsteadily on his feet. His attention was divided between the threatening

Campbell and the sudden, unexpected appearance of LouEtta.

Campbell didn't know what was taking place between Jeremiah and the black woman. But his stare bored into the face of the sweating Bridges.

"All right," he said, "I believe you will." With a parting glare at Bridges, and a nod to Jeremiah, Campbell turned on a heel and was gone.

Jeremiah turned to where he looked into the face of his wife.

Her eyes were misty, her hands trembled. To her, his voice was a hoarse whisper. "What are you doing in this house?" he said.

"I–I–live here, Jeremiah."

"You live here? With him? You clean his house?"

"Well, I–" LouEtta cried. "It's hard to–"

An evil chuckle escaped the lips of Simon Bridges. In the beginning he didn't know LouEtta was Jeremiah's wife. By the time he found out, he thought it no longer mattered.

Bridges had needed a housekeeper. Scanning the faces of the new arrivals, he chose LouEtta because of her pleasing appearance, and her experience as a domestic in Logantree's Big House. The emotional relationship evolved over time.

LouEtta, weary of resisting his advances, finally yielded to his demands.

"She's my woman, Higgins," Bridges said.

"Your woman?" Jeremiah couldn't believe it.

"Jeremiah, please," LouEtta pleaded tearfully. "I thought—I--I looked for you. I thought I'd never see you again."

Jeremiah was trying to straighten out in his mind exactly what the situation was. While he was doing the bidding of Simon Bridges, Bridges was hiding his wife in the house on the hill, making a slave of her, and– He wasn't sure he wanted to know what else.

"Leave her alone, Higgins," Bridges said. "She belongs to me now."

"You stay out of this," Jeremiah said. "This ain't your business."

"Like hell it ain't my business! Are you too blind to see? She don't want you anymore!"

"She's my wife," Jeremiah said. "The mother of my sons. She is not your woman!"

"I had no money, Jeremiah," LouEtta cried. "I couldn't let the boys go without."

"You brought my sons into this house?"

Bridges eyed the gun on the floor at his feet, itching to grab it and turn it on Jeremiah, but he was unsure he could reach it ahead of Jeremiah.

"Where are the boys now?" Jeremiah said.

"In school in Denver," LouEtta said.

"In school?"

"Mr. Bridges--he sent them to the academy."

Questions crowded Jeremiah's mind, answers to which he wasn't sure he wanted to hear. "You ain't his housemaid?"

LouEtta cast an anxious glance at Bridges, giving no answer.

"You dumb nigger!" Bridges jeered. "If it hadn't been for me they'd have starved to death."

"I thank you for that," Jeremiah said, hoarse with anger.

"Without my help," Bridges went on, "you'd still be busting your back on some hardscrabble farm in Mississippi." He extended a hand in a conciliatory gesture. "Come on, Higgins. We've been through too much together for this. You've been in my home, eaten at my table."

"In your kitchen, Mr. Bridges, not at your table." With a curious cock of his head, Jeremiah said, "Times when I was here, where was she?"

Bridges made a move toward the gun, but Jeremiah kicked it out of his reach. He struck him a vicious blow to the head. Bridges fell against the wall.

Jeremiah picked up the gun and aimed it at the groveling overseer.

Bridges threw up his hands in a feeble attempt to defend himself, nursing his bleeding mouth.

"Don't move or I'll kill you," Jeremiah said.

Bridges called upon all the bravado he could muster, and screamed, "You stupid nigger! You want to go back to Mississippi and scratch around in the dirt, working for yams and peanuts?"

"No, sir. But if you move I'm still gonna kill you."

To LouEtta, he said, "I'm leavin' now. I want you to come with me. We work this out somehow. We go to Denver to see the boys and start all over some place. We ain't slaves no more, LouEtta. Ain't nobody can tell us what to do. We make our own way and our own life." Holding the gun on Bridges, he started backing toward the door.

"LouEtta?" he said. "You comin', LouEtta?"

She covered her face with both hands, and wept.

Bridges made a sudden lunge at him. Jeremiah pulled the trigger. Bridges plopped to the floor, hugging his stomach.

LouEtta screamed, rushed to the fallen Bridges and knelt beside him. She cradled his head in her arms, and wiped his bleeding mouth with her head scarf.

Jeremiah was stunned. Heartsick and disappointed, that Bridges spoke the truth. LouEtta, caressing the face of the wounded overseer, no longer wanted to be his. There, sobbing bitter tears, knelt the wife for whom he searched half his life, only to find that she now belonged to someone else.

# CHAPTER EIGHTEEN

Jeremiah stared at the red brick structure someone told him was Lincoln Academy for boys. Except for the Big House on Logantree's plantation, he never saw such a tall building. Three stories high it was, with windows all around. Swarms of young black men, arms laden with books, scurried past him on their way to some place, as if they couldn't wait to get there.

Jeremiah had parked his wagon beside other wagons and buggies and tethered horses, and tied his team to the hitch rack in front of the building. Apprehensive, he approached the entrance and was swept inside by the wave of chattering students. The hallway was jammed with boys going in all directions, laughing and shouting at each other, ignoring the confused black man in their midst.

Jeremiah removed his black knit wool cap and twisted it in his hands. Almost, he wished he hadn't come. But in his eagerness to see his boys, it took him six days in the wagon to get to Denver. He couldn't turn back now. He needed to sit down with Jacob and Joseph and tell them what happened to him since he saw them last, and try to explain about their mother. It would be a hard time, but he told himself it had to be done.

He was startled by the clang of a bell and the rush of slamming doors. The hallway was suddenly empty. He was alone, engulfed by bewildering silence. He caught sight of a door standing open in the hallway. He made his feet move in that direction. Through the door he saw a chest-high counter. Behind the counter a young black man sat at a desk shuffling papers. Beyond the young man, at another, larger, desk sat an older black man with gray whiskers and wire rimmed spectacles.

Jeremiah shuffled into the room. Both men looked up from their desks with curious gazes.

"Yes?" the young man said, stepping to the counter.

"My–my boys," Jeremiah said.

"Your boys?"

"Jacob. Jacob and Joseph."

The young man cast a questioning glance at the older man at the desk behind him. The man with the gray whiskers got up from his desk and came to the counter. The younger man went back to his desk and began shuffling more papers. He shot a guarded glance toward the man at the counter.

"Is there something I can help you with?" the older man said to Jeremiah. He pushed his spectacles farther onto his nose.

"My boys," Jeremiah said again. "I need to see my boys."

"And who, sir, are your boys?"

"Jacob and Joseph."

"Jacob and Joseph," the man said. He studied the anxious face of the man awaiting his response. He suspected he was a former slave. If so, it was not likely the boys had a last name. Many children born into slavery did not. The parents of those who had last names often adopted the name of their master.

Not so with Jeremiah Higgins. His father chose the name of a white man who once visited the plantation and was kind to him.

"Well now, let me see," said the man with the gray whiskers. He turned to a cabinet on his left and brought out a ledger containing a list of names. He flipped through the pages till he found what he was looking for.

"Ah yes," he said, "here we are. Are you Mr. Higgins?"

"Yes, sir. Jeremiah Higgins." His heart leaped at the prospect of having found his sons.

The man turned with a look at the younger man shuffling papers at the desk. For a long moment they stared at each other.

"I'm afraid I have bad news for you, sir," the man behind the counter said.

"Bad news?"

"A few weeks ago, in the boarding house to which your sons were assigned, there was a serious fire."

With a sinking heart Jeremiah waited for the man to go on, not sure he wanted to hear what else he had to say. But he had to know.

"Several of our young men were lost in the fire," the man said. "We don't know how it started."

Jeremiah had difficulty understanding what his ears were asking him to believe. "My boys–they die?" he said.

"I'm so sorry, sir."

Jeremiah responded with a sorrowful nod. His eyes clouded with tears, his hands gave his cap a fierce twist.

"My boys die," he said. With a solemn nod, he said again, "My boys die." At the door on his way out, he paused. "I thank you, sir," he said. He pulled on his black wool cap, and went out.

The men behind the counter watched him go. The dejected man who searched for all those years, and traveled six days to get to where he was sure he'd find his sons, finally did.

Jeremiah climbed onto the wagon seat, took up the reins and flicked the team forward. With a heavy heart, he began the lonely drive back to Nicodemus.

# CHAPTER NINETEEN

Down Jeremiah's neck and onto his bare chest, rolls of sweat soaked the tops of his cotton pants. He was shaping a slab of metal into a plowshare he promised a farmer he'd have done that day. Never had he given less than everything he had to whatever he did, no matter the task. And he couldn't recall, even in his slave days on the plantation, working harder, nor longer, than he pushed himself in recent weeks.

It wasn't only his promise to the farmer that kept him doggedly at the anvil. He needed to work, work hard and long, long enough to ease the pain of losing his sons, unable as he was to see them before they died in the fire. Denied the joy of holding them close as he once did, he wanted them to know how much he loved them, to let them know he did search for them and their mother. For thirteen years. Time would be used up before he sweated enough to wash away the hurt and sorrow of losing them all.

What took place in the Big House of Simon Bridges would forever haunt him. In the middle of the night he was jarred awake by the nightmare, staring into the condemning night, agonizing over why LouEtta no longer wanted him.

If only he'd found her in his travels, things would be different. The sadness and disappointment would be blocked out by the joy of being together.

There were times he wished he had killed Bridges instead of only wounding him with the gun shot. Times, too, when, completely bewildered, he shivered with the realization of how close he came to shooting LouEtta. Even in anger, though, and the state of near insanity that swept over him at the time, he could have done nothing to harm her. She was his wife, the mother of his children. But she made her choice. It didn't include him.

Rachel was waiting for him when he returned from Denver. She asked about the boys. She cried when he told her they died in the fire. She had always brought with her a ray of sunshine that brightened the shadows. Now she was sad.

With so many things closing in on him, Jeremiah hadn't made up his mind about her.

"What you gon do now, Big Boy?" she asked him.

He took a moment to find the right words. "I been thinkin' 'bout that. What I decided is I--I ain't decided nothin' yet. But I be needin' some help. Where you reckon I--maybe find somebody to--put me back together--so's I be a whole man again?"

"I be here, Big Boy." With a small smile she

pressed his hand to her cheek. "I be here."

# ABOUT THE AUTHOR

David Estes is an accomplished author with seven books to his credit. He draws on his wide experience, from the cotton fields of Oklahoma and Texas where he grew up; to the islands of the South Pacific where he served as a United States Marine; to the marketplace in America where he pursued a career in radio and television advertising. Now retired, David writes westerns and mystery novels from his family farm in West Central Missouri.

# OTHER PUBLICATIONS BY DAVID A. ESTES

Available at Amazon.com, Barnes&Noble.com, Booksamillion.com and more online retailers.

Bag of Gold
Blood on the Wall
Bye Bye, Sweet Susie
Angel on My Back
Wet Dogs Don't Ride
Ajax & Elbow Grease

DAVID A. ESTES